STIRRING

BOOK TWO OF THE EMBLEM AND THE LANTERN

OR

THE JOURNEY OF THE EMBLEM

DYLAN HIGGINS

First Edition: Hill Harow Books: August 2012

The characters and events portrayed in this book are fictitious. Any
similarity to real persons, living or dead, is coincidental and not intended
by the author, unless permission has been granted.

Library of Congress Cataloging-in-Publication Data

Dylan Higgins.
    Stirring: Book Two of The Emblem and The Lantern / by Dylan
Higgins; Illustrated by Mikael Jury.
    1st ed.
    ISBN 13: 978-1475263039
    ISBN 10: 1475263031
    This is a work of literary fiction.
                Edited by Joanna Jury and Barbara Toth.
                The text was set in Palatino.

This book is for my son, Ethan. Truth is knowable! Wisdom is obtainable!

"Where is the one who is wise? Where is the scribe? Where is the debater of this age? Has not God made foolish the wisdom of the world?" (1 Corinthians 1:20)

CONTENTS

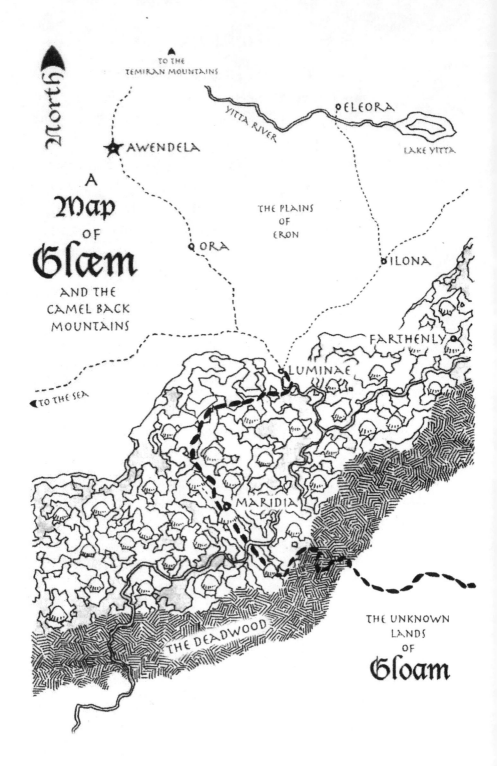

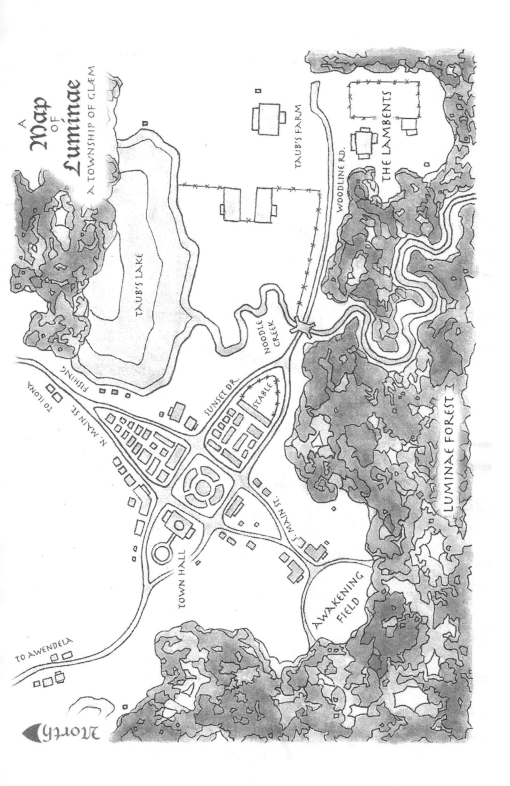

A Map of Luminae
A TOWNSHIP OF GLÆM

TAUB'S LAKE

TAUB'S FARM

WOODLINE RD.

THE LAMBENTS

NOODLE CREEK

LUMINÆ FOREST

FISHING

TO ILONA

N. MAIN ST.

SUNSET DR.

STABLE

S. MAIN ST.

TOWN HALL

AWAKENING FIELD

TO AWENDELA

North

Those with wings, be it bird or beast...

Prologue

Far north of Glæm lie the snow-covered Temiran Mountains whose colossal icy peaks are so unreachable that no man has ever gazed upon their splendor. These frozen monuments of creation are home only to creatures of flight that roost near the ceiling of the world, or the floor of the heavens, depending upon one's view of things.

However, the inhabitants of these mountains find themselves baffled at present. Before their wondering eyes something stirs-- a lone figure exits a cave in the heights of the rocky crags. Those with wings, be it bird or beast, fly in circling patterns, high above the mysterious traveler. They watch as the cloaked one makes his way carefully down, down, down a trail that had, until now, remained a secret. His destination is unknown to those who watch from high above.

Chapter One
The First Morning

Flying...flying across a barren wasteland on the back of the sun. This is how it appeared to Ethan Lambent as his eyes adjusted to the bright light emanating from within the immense creature he rode upon. While very much lost in his own thoughts, the young man was not alone. He was accompanied by his twin sister Eisley who sat just behind him, holding tight to his waist. He and Eisley had just been on an amazing and perilous adventure together. With the help of the Magic Lantern and the Light within it, the siblings overcame the ancient evil called Smarr, and his minions, the Watchers.

There were others who faced the darkness with the twins, as well. Their mother, Evangeline, and their father, Amory, journeyed to Gloam to find and rescue their children, joined by Grandpa Emmett and Grandma Jaine. Also, Deerborn, Captain of the Maridian Guard, left his wife, Abril, and his home, in Maridia, to aide Ethan and Eisley on their quest. Canis, the former Watcher, helped the twins, too, risking his life in a desperate fight against his fellow Watchers who endeavored to destroy the Magic Lantern and the Glæmians possessing it. Canis lay limp in the arms of Grandma Jaine. The extent of the price he had paid to help Ethan and Eisley was not yet known. Lastly, at the call of the Magic Lantern, the Camel Back Mountains had come to life in the form of illuminated behemoths called Ancients. They were the ones who finally overcame Smarr. After the monster was subdued, one of the Ancients revealed that the Lambent family, "would be called upon to harness the power of the Light and put an end to Smarr" in time. Now the Lambents sat, nestled, in a cleft on the neck of the very Ancient who had spoken these words. They watched in wonder as the shining creature beat its massive outstretched wings in long, powerful strokes, each taking them further away from danger.

Together the Lambents, Deerborn and Canis, flew over Gloam's first morning. Using a dark magic, Smarr had held equally dark clouds in place above Gloam for ages, casting a seemingly eternal night over the country's inhabitants. Now, that thick oppression was vanquished, and light flooded the land. Finally, the Gloamers would see for the first time and begin to understand that the Light was life. No longer would they have to be slaves to darkness.

Below the flying travelers lay mile upon mile of desert. Behind them lay Smarr, dormant and still, like the mountain he had been before he'd uprooted and attacked the Lambents. Smarr was fettered to the ground now. How long the Ancients' power would contain him was unknown. Ethan hoped it would be years because he knew that the creature's mind was racing with wicked intent whose focus was on he and his family. He could still hear Smarr's voice in his mind telling him that he was more like the darkness than the Light. Smarr's deceiving power had nearly caused Ethan to become one with the darkness, to become a servant of Evil. Yet, by the work of pure providence, Ethan had awakened and believed in the Creator without a moment to spare. He had burst into light, eye to eye with Smarr, shining goodness into the face of evil. The young Glæmian was not ready to face such arrant furry again anytime soon. The encounter nearly cost him his life and, even worse, it nearly cost him his soul.

The travelers were now above the Deadwood, and passing over it much faster than they traversed through it. The gray, dead trees soon gave way to the green, vibrant life of Luminae Forest. The Ancient began to slow, descending toward Maridia's Eastern Lookout: a mountain bordering the Deadwood. As they drew close to the mountaintop watchtower, Deerborn let out a cry. On the uppermost level of the tower stood his wife, Abril, whose white dress billowed in the wind of the Ancient's wings. She stood unafraid. Either the Ancient had spoken to her by thought, easing her mind, or she had seen her husband on the creature's back. The Ancient reached a mighty earthen-arm up toward its passengers allowing Deerborn to crawl into its opened, glowing talons.

"Farewell my brave friends," said the man, tearfully, as he passed Ethan and Eisley.

"Will we ever see you again?" asked Eisley through tears of her own.

"I'm sure of it," answered Deerborn, sinking towards the lookout. "One day, soon, I will find my way to your land..."

But then his voice was drowned out by the beating of the Ancient's wings.

Deerborn was placed carefully upon the tower and the Lambents watched as the man ran to Abril, lifting her high off the ground like an athlete might raise his prized trophy. The lovers smiled wide through their joyful tears.

Ethan and Eisley waved to Deerborn and Abril, who waved in return, and with a forward surge the Ancient was on the move again, heading west.

Traveling on, the Lambents saw that all the other Ancients had not come back to their roosts. Gaping holes speckled the canopy of the forest. Where had they gone after defeating Smarr? The Ancients had most certainly raced off into the west, back towards the forest. Yet, nearly every one of them was missing now. All but a few were scattered over the horizon; the closest ones being the mountains that Maridia and the two lookouts sat upon.

Soon, Ethan saw smoke rising from the chimneys of warm homes across Luminae Township. As they neared, he saw Town Hall, he saw Awakening Field, and he saw home.

"Ethan!" shouted Eisley.

Ethan couldn't understand why his sister was shouting. She was sitting just behind him.

"Ethan!"

"Cut it out!" said Ethan.

Then something peculiar happened. The landscape surrounding Luminae started to ripple and vanish and everything turned white.

"Wake up!"

Ethan opened his eyes. Above him was a very familiar ceiling. The sun's first rays poured through his bedroom window. He had been dreaming.

Chapter Two

Things Which Have and Have Not Been

"Wake up, sleepy head!" said Eisley, standing in the doorway. "We've been over this before. If you're going to run with me, you have to get up earlier than this!"

Eisley tied her wavy hair back in a ponytail. She smirked at Ethan as he sat up and rubbed the sleep from his eyes. His mind was a blur. Had it all been a dream? Maridia? Gloam? Smarr? To be sure, he peered over at his desk. If it had been a dream then the unfinished map would not be lying there. But there it was, the sketch of what would one day be a detailed map of Gloam, depicting his and his sister's journey.

Eisley's smirk turned to a look of concern. "The same dream again?"

"Yeah," said Ethan, running his fingers through his hair.

"Of the trip home?" asked Eisley, sitting down on the bed next to her brother.

Ethan nodded.

"I wonder why you keep dreaming about it?"

"Who knows?" replied Ethan, standing to shake off the sleep.

Dreams had consumed his waking thoughts for weeks, and with good reason. In the past, Ethan had dreamt of things that would eventually become reality, like dreams of Gloamers peering at him through the darkness and dreams of his family battling alongside he and Eisley in a dark land. Then there was the dream that hadn't come to pass-- the one where the Magic Lantern changed into an emblem that resembled the lantern. He'd asked about the emblem around town and searched the library for information, but without luck. No one had ever heard of such an emblem. The dream had only come to him once, but it remained vivid in his mind.

More recently, though, his nights had been filled with dreams of past events, like the one of him and his family flying home on the Ancient. He'd had this dream every night of the past cycle of Vergance, Glæm's greatest moon. He thought about the dream. He thought about the empty roosts of the Ancients in Luminae Forest. He knew now why the mountains hadn't returned to the wood. Just the day before, the Lambents received news that the Camel Back Mountains were surrounding Awendela, the capital of Glæm. Luminae was buzzing with talk of the anomaly. But as of yet none knew what the mountains really were, none but the Lambents and the twins' other grandparents, Charston and Noemi Hale. The Hales knew everything now. They knew that Riley, the Boy of Legend, was a Lambent ancestor and they knew about his lantern, the Magic Lantern, that now belonged to Ethan and Eisley's family.

"Are you ready?" asked Eisley, shaking Ethan from his reverie.

"Let's go!" replied Ethan fastening the last strap of his shoe.

Ever since they returned from their adventure, Ethan could not sit still for very long. He'd gotten so used to staying on his feet day after day that he found it necessary to continue doing so. He'd become nearly as quick as his sister, and Eisley hadn't minded at all, even as competitive as she was. She and her brother had become so attached to one another on their journey that they spent nearly every waking moment together. Few Glæmians knew the kind of bond that springs from two people having weathered a significant storm together, such as the twins had experienced.

As brother and sister ran through the center of Luminae township, a few of the shop owners ogled from their windows, eyeing the twins with curiosity. It was well known that Ethan and Eisley disappeared into the forest and were gone for several months. No one in Luminae knew where they had gone to and, for the most part, they remained disinterested. But, the town became more curious when the twins' parents and grandparents also disappeared.

Naturally, rumors spread. Some people wondered if the Lambents had gotten caught up in the stories of the Boy of Legend. There was no rational explanation for why this rumor would be true, though. *Most* didn't believe that the old stories had ever actually happened and *none* knew the true identity of Riley Lambent. So there was no reason to think the Lambents had been party to such foolishness.

Soon, the twins completed their run. As they turned off the road into their yard, they heard their father shout from behind the house.

"Hey, Ethan, Galby's gotten out of the pen again! Can you get him?"

"Yes, sir," replied Ethan, begrudgingly.

"And Eisley," said Amory, "Mom needs help in the kitchen."

"I'm on my way," said Eisley, leaping on to the porch.

"Late start today, huh?" teased their father, coming around the side of the house.

"Talk to your son about that," said Eisley opening the screen door.

"Sorry," said Ethan. "I didn't sleep very well."

"That's becoming a bit of a routine," said Ethan's father, wrapping his arms around his son.

Ethan soaked in his father's embrace. He thought back to a time, months earlier, when there was still a chance that such an embrace might never happen again.

"Go on son," said Amory, kindly. "Go get that hard-headed goat back in his pin and try to be quick about it, there's plenty of chores to do."

Though he was already running behind schedule, Ethan wasted more time chasing Galby the goat around the yard. Finally he managed to wrestle the animal back into its pin. Like his father had said there were chores still to do. While becoming an adult in the land of Glæm brought a newfound sense of respect, it also brought a new sense of responsibility. The twins had become a working part of the community. Every morning they tended to their horses, Lewis and Lucy. Then they'd go across the road to help Mr. Taubs with all of his livestock, milking the cows, checking on the processing cheeses, and the many other things that needed doing on a profitable dairy farm. Mr. Taubs owned more land than anyone in Luminae and was always in need of help. As Glæm rested on the brink of spring, there was other farming to do. The time had come to weed and till the fields. The Lambents grew potatoes and other edible roots, as did many in those parts. Besides the daily chores, Ethan and Eisley were called to help others in the community from time to time, like when a new home needed to be built or a family needed extra food. The town always shared their resources when need arose.

Of course, the chores were voluntary for Ethan and Eisley. At adulthood they were given the option to continue their education, but the siblings had opted out for the time being. Eisley had never been excited about the idea of school, which is why her decision had come as no surprise. But Amory and Evangeline were shocked to discover that Ethan didn't want to go to university. It was all he'd ever dreamed of. Secretly, Ethan was waiting for the right time to tell his parents that he was going back to Maridia to accept an offer that had been made to him there.

He gazed up at her, one eye looking much bigger than the other...

Chapter Three
Stirring

"Grandpa's here; he says Canis is well enough to see Luminae now!" said Eisley, entering Ethan's room. Ethan sat hunched over his desk, tongue sticking out, which occurred whenever he was deep in thought. Eisley giggled. Her brother wore a funny looking contraption on his head-- a leather band with a mechanical arm attached to it, holding a magnifying glass in place over his right eye. His own invention.

"Finally!" said Ethan. He gazed up at her, one eye looking much bigger than the other through the magnifying glass. His expression brought a fresh wave of laughter to Eisley. Ethan joined. Nearing the desk, Eisley saw that he'd been drawing a wolf-like creature next to a tent on his map of Gloam. Above it, inscribed in fine lettering, was the phrase, 'Encounter with the Squalor.'

Ethan pushed the monocle up to his forehead and rose from his seat.

"Let's go see him!" he said.

The twins were stopped by Grandpa Emmett as they ran through the sitting room, headed toward the front door.

"Remember, Canis... looks and sounds different than we do. The town will notice."

"We know, Grandpa," said Ethan, interrupting Emmett.

"Hold on a sec, son," he continued, aggravated. "I know ya know. Just keep it in mind. The town's been leery of us since we got back. Them seein' Canis for the first time might not make things any easier."

"He can't stay in your house forever," said Eisley.

"No, 'course not, Eisley girl. Just be prepared. That's all I'm askin'."

"Yes, sir," said the twins in unison.

Since their return from Gloam, Canis had been cared for by Grandma Jaine. Emmett and Jaine lived on Main Street, just north of town, where their house burrowed up against the small wood lining the northern banks of Taub's Lake. It was in this home that Canis had been taught more about the Creator and had begun to believe in the Light. Canis' experience with the twins in Gloam had opened his eyes in a very literal sense. Though, he had already started down the path to belief. Even before he awakened, he defended the twins against his own kind, risking his very life. At the time, he hadn't fully understood what the twins believed but he had seen in them something pure and true.

Ethan and Eisley spent much of their free time with Canis while he healed. Canis contributed to Ethan's continuing education. During the winter months, Ethan had enthusiastically chronicled the culture and histories of Gloam through the stories Canis told him. He couldn't wait to show his findings[1] to Rector Osric, the head of Maridia's university.

---

[1] See End Notes, Reference #1

Ethan knew that Osric would appreciate his records more than anyone. But now, according to Grandpa Emmett, the Gloamer-turned-Glæmian was well enough to venture out into his new country.

Ethan and Eisley ran as fast as they could all the way to their grandparents' house. Rushing up to the little stone cottage, they ran through the front door. Canis stood tall and healthy and ready to go. He looked much like he had the first time they'd seen him. A few things were different, though. His hair was cut shorter, shorter even than Ethan's, and he wore Glæmian clothing rather than Squalor fur.

"Are you ready?" asked Ethan.

Canis nodded expectantly. He looked excited. Like a child about to receive a present.

Together the three of them walked toward Luminae. As they passed the public fishing hole, Ethan thought about his grandpa's words. Ethan hoped that after seeing Canis, the townspeople would treat the Lambents as the heroes he thought they were-- just like those in Luminae had done with Riley so many centuries earlier. After all, they had brought back a Gloamer like Riley had.

"Just like old times, huh?" said Eisley.

"Um... it is a bit brighter, I think," said Canis in his singsong voice.

The three laughed as they neared the town.

Canis was enjoying himself thoroughly but as they strolled down the sidewalk on Main toward the square, Ethan's apprehension grew. Thus far, no one had paid them any mind but Ethan feared this wouldn't last. The twins pointed out the different shops they passed-- Bon's Bakery, the Tailor's shop, the Silversmith. They crossed the road into the square, the grassy center of town, that, only months ago, housed the stages for the annual Awakening Festival. Now it was empty.

"What is this building?" asked Canis, curiously pointing to the three-story structure on the far side of the square.

"That's Town Hall," said Ethan. "That's where our Elders meet to discuss Luminae's business."

"It is so beautiful," said Canis, squinting at the golden dome reflecting the sun's rays.

"If he likes this, I can't wait to see his reaction to the shining city," said Ethan to his sister.

Eisley grinned.

"Awendela is its proper name, correct?" asked Canis.

"That's right," answered Eisley. "We'll go there someday soon."

Ethan noticed a few people had congregated in the grass behind them. They were looking at Canis. When they saw that Ethan had noticed, they turned quickly in mock conversation.

Eisley looked at her brother, concerned.

Canis glanced over at the people. He waved at them but they did not return his greeting. Instead they walked off in huddled conversation.

"Hmm," said Canis curious about the people's reaction. "You *do* wave to say hello in Glæm, correct?"

"Yes, we do," grimaced Ethan.

"I thought so," said Canis. "Did I do it the wrong way?"

"No," said Ethan unsure of how else to reply. He couldn't believe the townsfolk had just walked off without returning Canis' greeting. They were usually so welcoming.

"Oh, I know what we could do," said Eisley, changing the subject. "Let's take Canis down to Awakening Field."

"Where the ceremonies take place?" asked Canis. "I've been wanting to go there."

Ethan hadn't thought about what importance Awakening Field might hold for Canis, who had just awakened himself. The field was a place the Lambents usually avoided. But for someone who hadn't grown up near it, Awakening Field probably seemed like an exciting place to visit.

Heading toward the field they passed all the strange shops on South Main that sold impractical items for the Awakening ceremonies. The door of one shop stood beneath a garish sign which Canis slowly read aloud, "Personalize Your Awakening Experience with Percival's Personalized Plaques!" He'd been learning to read and was getting pretty good for such little training.

Eisley snickered and rolled her eyes at the sign.

They didn't notice, but as they walked on, some of the townsfolk began to trail behind them. When they reached Awakening Field, Ethan explained the ceremony to Canis. He pointed towards the scattered entrances along the edge of the tall, thick wood. These openings looked similar to the mouths of caves. Ethan shared that the many wooded archways led to clearings where the children would go with their lanterns to spend the night. The three heard talking behind them and turned to see that a small crowd had formed, all eyes on Canis.

"Hello," said Ethan, anxiously.

The townsfolk said nothing at first. Ethan recognized most of the people but he only knew a few by name. Among the onlookers stood Elder Alem, who had evidently followed them from Town Hall, where he worked. A woman he knew named Eima spoke up.

"Who's your guest, Ethan?" she asked, shortly.

"This is Canis," Ethan replied.

Ethan was grateful someone had finally said something, even if he didn't particularly approve of Eima's tone.

"Hullo," answered Canis, nearly singing the word.

Some of the bystanders gasped.

"Hello, Canis, is it?" said Elder Alem, rigidly. "Might I ask where you are from? Your accent is unfamiliar to me. North of the Yitta River perhaps?"

Ethan didn't like were this was going.

Canis' voice took on a darker tone, almost like a song in a minor key. "I am from Gloam."

This time everyone gasped. Then angry statements started erupting from the crowd. "Did you bring him here?!" one shouted. "He's so strange looking! So pale!" said another. Their voices rose and fell in a head-pounding chorus. Ethan was confused by what was happening and he was growing angry.

"What's the matter with you all?" he exclaimed. The chorus fizzled. "Yes! Canis is from Gloam! He came back with us! That's right. We were there too! He saved our lives. Didn't he Eisley?"

Eisley didn't answer. With tears in his eyes Ethan looked around for his sister, but she was nowhere to be seen. "Eisley?"

"You say he came back with you? Where has he been since you returned? Why have we not seen him yet?" asked Elder Alem.

"He's been living with my grandparents. They've been nursing him back to health!" he explained.

A look of anger filled the people's faces.

"Why do you look so upset? He's awakened! He believes as we do! "

No one spoke.

"Didn't the Boy of Legend bring Gloamers back from the darkness?"

"He wasn't real! Everyone knows that!" said Eima.

They really *didn't* believe in Riley.

"Then what is all this for?" Ethan pointed at Awakening Field. "If the Boy of Legend wasn't real, then why even bother with the ceremony?"

Some people glared at him; some looked down as if to ponder his question.

The tense silence was broken by the galloping of horses coming down the way. The crowd shifted as Amory and Eisley galloped up on Lewis and Lucy. Eisley had run home to get their father.

"Whoa, girl!" said Eisley to her horse, Lucy.

Amory assessed the scene. "You should all be ashamed of your behavior."

"What business did you have in Gloam, Amory?" asked Elder Alem.

"My business is my own. Come on, Ethan," said Amory sternly. It didn't sound as if his tone was directed at Ethan, but rather at the crowd. "You too, Canis."

Ethan climbed up behind Eisley, Canis, behind Amory.

"You shouldn't have gone, Amory. He shouldn't be here," said someone in the crowd.

"We will discuss this another time," replied Amory.

He guided the horse by the reigns and yelled, "Yah!" Lewis was off, Lucy followed. They raced toward the center of town where more people had congregated. The argument had brought the town out into the streets. As they turned east on to Woodline Road, headed for home, Ethan thought the crowd resembled angry little hornets, having just been stirred from their nest.

Chapter Four
Vergance and His Brothers

By dinner almost everyone's mood was back to normal. The Lambent family sat with their celebrated guest Canis, and enjoyed a meal of meat and potato stew with kettle cakes. Despite the good food and cheerful company, Ethan couldn't shake the afternoon's events. In the middle of a story Eisley had been telling in one of her silly voices (that she hadn't made since she was little), Ethan dropped his eating utensil with a loud CLANG and slid his chair back forcefully from the table.

Eisley stopped talking and all eyes fell on Ethan.

"How can you ignore what's happening?" he shouted, storming toward the front door.

He heard his mother say his name as a worried mother might. As he shoved open the door he heard his father say, "Just let him go, love."

Ethan slammed the screen door and tromped out into the twilight, glaring skyward. Vergance, the largest moon, began to sink below the horizon. Yet, his brother Miland, the second largest, and Ancelin, the smallest of the three, stood high and proud in the sky above. As was always the case in Glæm, two of the three brothers shone brightly in the sky at all times, bringing light even through the night. He turned toward the dark part of the sky where any visible stars would be, and there he saw the constellation Artan, the little bear, that appeared to chase the brother moons across the sky.

"You know," said Amory, startling Ethan as he joined his son, "the Celestions are saying that the moons and the sun will all align with us. Grandpa says that hasn't happened in over a millennium. It's expected to happen sometime in the coming months."

Ethan didn't speak but he was very interested in the phenomenon. The study of the heavens was a subject that Ethan, Amory and Emmett equally enjoyed.[2] Having seen a few partial eclipses before, Ethan often wondered if a total alignment was even possible.

Amory stroked his bushy beard making the scratchy noise that Ethan's mother disliked immensely. It usually meant his father was pondering something very deeply.

"You can't judge the Creator by His creation, Ethan," said Amory. "People are not perfect, only the Light is."

Ethan smiled for the first time that evening. Clearly, talk of the moons had been an ice-breaker. He knew the truth of his father's words; the only perfect thing was the Light. It was what led to him believing in the Creator in the first place.

"I just don't understand how people with the Light in them can be so uncaring and hateful?" Ethan asked as he finally looked at his father.

"Yes... that seems problematic doesn't it, my boy?" Amory sighed, thoughtful. "However, the Light has given all people

---

2 See End Notes, Reference #2

the ability to know what is right. Sometimes, I dare say most of the time, we choose to do otherwise. He's given us that ability as well."

Ethan wondered how his father was able to remain so calm about the situation. With all that had happened that day, compulsion got the best of him.

"Speaking of choices," began Ethan. "I've decided to go back to Maridia."

"Hmm... your mother and I thought this might happen."

"You did?"

"You're constantly talking about that town-- Deerborn and his wife, that funny old Librarian, Jukes and... Delia, is it?" Amory grinned. Ethan looked away, a little embarrassed.

It was true Ethan had been talking about Maridia non-stop.

"You are a man now," said Amory. "You are free to do as you choose. Just choose wisely... you always have."

Ethan wasn't sure what his father meant, given the trouble he'd gotten himself and his sister into.

"Going to Gloam was not a mistake, son. Despite what you may think." Amory seemed to read Ethan's mind. "When the Ancient spoke the prophecy, concerning *us* ridding Gloam of Smarr's evil, I knew what you had done had been... destined."

There was momentary silence between them.

"I think we were all supposed to be there, Ethan... just as it happened." Amory ruffled Ethan's hair and walked back toward the house.

Ethan thought about his father's words in the silence of the moonlit evening. He knew the fight against Smarr had been the will of the Creator, with or without the prophecy. Ethan and Eisley both felt the overwhelming call into the darkness. The feeling of being drawn to Gloam left Ethan at the end of their journey, yet Eisley still felt a strong desire to reach the Gloamers she'd made friends with-- Nellek, Eecyak, and the others. In fact, had it not been for their need to treat Canis in safety, Eisley would have stayed in Gloam.

"You okay?" came the voice of Eisley sometime later. She came to stand where her father had.

"I'm fine," said Ethan. "I told Father that I was going back to Maridia."

"How did he take it?" asked Eisley. She already knew about his plan.

"Very well, actually."

"Well... good," said Eisley, gazing skyward now like her brother. "I wonder what they'll say of me going back to Gloam?"

"That will be a completely different talk, I believe," laughed Ethan. The thought of their father willingly allowing his baby girl to go into Gloam again was almost absurd.

"Yes, I think it will be," replied Eisley. "I'll wait a while before I tell them. You've probably surprised them enough for the time being."

"I will go with you," said Canis.

Ethan and Eisley jumped as they turned to see that Canis was standing behind them. The new Glæmian was still as quiet as a Gloamer.

"My people need to know the truth."

Together the three friends stood and silently watched Vergance sink below the horizon.

Two unlikely visitors and a strange little creature....

Chapter Five
Of Hosts and House Guests

Time passed by in the land of Glæm. Seeds were planted and the fields began to yield their harvest. Spring was giving way to summer. This change in weather would normally lead to lazy afternoons on the front porch swing with glasses of cold tea in hand; which, usually, would be accompanied by calm, reflective thoughts. For some, those thoughts were meanderings of the agrarian sort-- what to plant next, or when to leave the cool of the shade to water the crops. For others, thoughts of the coming autumn prevailed. Fall was the busiest time of year for those in Luminae because of the Awakening ceremony. Plans were being made even now to make this year's Awakening bigger and better than all that had come before. This is how the planners thought every year. And there were those who'd been thinking of making the pilgrimage to Luminae for the ceremony. People would soon begin to leave their homes from far and wide to come and participate in the celebration. These were the kinds of things that most folk in the land of light had on their minds; but not the Lambents.

Since Ethan's outburst in town, all of Luminae stirred with talk of the newcomer. Ethan and Eisley's parents and grandparents had been arguing with the town elders in defense of Canis' right to stay in Glæm. The elders believed that Canis' presence would somehow taint their way of life.

The Lambents fought vehemently on Canis' behalf, citing that the Boy of Legend brought many from the land of Gloam into their midst and the town had welcomed them with open arms. Most of the elders countered this by acknowledging that the Boy of Legend was nothing more than legend, and that Gloamers had probably never assimilated into Glæm's society. The Lambents knew that Riley was real. Evangeline had suggested revealing the Magic Lantern to the town. Grandpa Emmett swore up and down that the townsfolk would make a mockery of the Lambent heirloom rather than revere it for the artifact it was. "Mark my words," he told the family one day, "if there's that many of 'em thinkin' that Riley ain't real, then they won't believe the Lantern for what it is either!" And so the Lambents could only argue on moral grounds. Amory stood before the elders and said, "All men have the right to live in Glæm, especially if they believe as we do." The Lambents continually reminded the elders that Canis had Awakened, yet it did no good. The elders seemed to think that Canis' reformation wasn't genuine. Impossible even.

The whole ordeal became quite absurd. Ethan and Eisley began to keep to themselves, staying home with Canis who had come to live with them, while Luminae kept up their protests.

It was in this unfortunate state that two unlikely visitors and a strange little creature made their way into town one day. Locals had seen this burly, red-headed man and the fair lady that traveled with him exiting the Luminae Forest due west of town. Some watched from windows with wary expressions as the strangers wandered into the square and began to inquire as to the whereabouts of the Lambent residence. Being so broad-shouldered and bear-like, the man had received the information he sought without any trouble. And so it was that one dewy morning, Deerborn, Captain of the Maridian Guard, his wife, Abril, and their pet D'mune, a squat, furry little creature resembling a mix between a potato and a rat, came strolling into the Lambents' front yard.

Amory, the twins and Canis were on their knees weeding the garden. Eisley thought she'd seen something out of the corner of her eye.

"Ho, Lambents!" shouted Deerborn.

"Deerborn! Abril!" exclaimed Eisley, standing from her grimy work. She ran to the burly man. Most of the dirt covering her was transferred to the recipient of her embrace, though Deerborn didn't seem to notice at all. The big man lifted Eisley from the ground with ease and spun her around, laughing as he did. He set the young woman down next to Abril who eagerly enveloped her in a motherly sort of hug. Ethan came running up shortly after to embrace Deerborn and Abril in much the same fashion as his sister. Eisley now on her back, having been playfully attacked by the D'mune named Poudis. The little creature ran back and forth along Eisley's torso, shuddering comically with excitement.

"Greetings, travelers!" said Amory through a big bushy grin that reflected his guest's.

Evangeline came out of the house to see what all of the commotion was about and affectionately greeted the visitors ,as well.

"What brings you to our neck of the woods?" asked Amory.

"Well, we told Ethan and Eisley that we'd visit their home some day and...here we are," said Deerborn. "Truth be told, we just missed the brave rascals!"

Everyone laughed.

"I do hope we aren't imposing on you," said Abril.

"Of course not," said Evangeline. "Your husband put himself in harm's way for our children. You could never impose on us."

Canis lingered near the edge of the garden watching the reunion with an amused sort look on his face. Deerborn noticed him standing back and with narrowed eyes said, "Canis? Could it be the same Gloamer who lay lifeless in the arms of Jaine Lambent when last I saw him?"

"One and the same," said Evangeline.

Deerborn moved slowly towards Canis, as one might a new acquaintance, and introduced himself, then Abril and Poudis. The latter sniffed at Canis' feet. Canis, in turn, sung out his own name and clasped arms with the Maridian as he'd seen Amory do moments earlier-- the new Glæmian was still getting used to the strange customs.

"Well met," said Deerborn through a hearty laugh. "Well met, indeed!"

Evangeline ushered the travel weary guests into the house, eager to refresh them. Eisley was sent to gather her grandparents from their home, knowing they, too, would be pleased to see Deerborn and Abril.

That evening the Lambent home was filled with much frivolity. The group enjoyed many a song and dance as well as a great feast from the recent harvest. There was roasted corn on the cob and savory collards to be eaten with golden-browned cornbread. There were sweets, as well-- puddings, pastries with pudding in them and more than could possibly be eaten. To crown the occasion, Amory and Emmett smoked a succulent pig, putting it to the most noble use it could ever hope to have: the sustenance of mankind. All in all, the evening turned out to be a much needed time of celebration for the otherwise weary-hearted family.

Chapter Six

An Uneasy Feeling

"It's so wonderful having you here, Abril," sighed Eisley.

"Aye, young one, it is good to be here," said Abril, "and to get to know your family."

Deerborn and Abril had fallen right into step with the Lambents' daily routines after their arrival. Abril helped Evangeline peel potatoes at the kitchen table. Eisley was behind her, fiddling with her hair, and was in better spirits than she had been in a while. Abril's presence had been just as Eisley imagined it would be. Deerborn's wife and Evangeline were very similar. Though Abril was a few years younger, Eisley knew that the two would get along well together. Evangeline had seen Abril only briefly and from afar when the Ancient had dropped Deerborn off at the Eastern Lookout. But now it was as if the two had known each other their whole lives.

While the ladies held light-hearted conversation about the supper they were preparing, the men's talk was of a wholly other sort in the yard where they resumed garden-weeding from the previous day. Ethan and Amory took turns filling Deerborn in on the recent happenings in Luminae. They shared with him all that had gone on since they'd last seen one another-- some good, like Canis' conversion (which

Deerborn was very interested in), and some bad, like the townsfolks' attitude toward Canis.

Canis worked quietly through all the talk. He felt somewhat guilty for the way the Lambents had been treated on his account. He knew that Ethan and Eisley's family were good people who would advocate for him to the very end.

"Hmph... people are hard to figure out sometimes," commented Deerborn.

"That they are," replied Amory.

Ethan looked up at his father and Deerborn as they concentrated hard on the task at hand. He shook his head in confusion. Yet again he was amazed at his father's ability to garner such peace of mind amid trying times like these. He hoped one day he'd inherit that ability from his father.

"There, that should do it," said Deerborn rising from the garden.

Shaking away the frustration, Ethan thought about how great it was to see Deerborn again. It was a bit surreal for the young man to see his protector and friend there, in his own garden, doing menial labor, being a soldier like he was. Ethan let his thoughts wander towards Maridia. He pondered what Rector Osric might be doing at present. Perhaps he was in his study preparing class lectures. Then his thoughts turned to Alaric Jukes, the Overseer of Maridia, and finally to his daughter, Delia. He'd begun to take a liking to Delia during his brief visit. He thought about how silly he felt the morning he first met her. He had hit the underside of the dining table at breakfast, causing all the pancakes to fly off their plate. He remembered how Delia cried when she found out he was going into Gloam, thinking he would never come back. And, with a blush he remembered how he kissed her on the cheek when they left. He wanted to see her again. He wanted to walk through the town of Maridia and visit the library with its books and its funny old keeper, Miss Naava. He was ready to go back to school and, more than anything, he was ready to get out of the hometown that had become as strange and foreign to him as Gloam had been.

Ethan looked up from his work again at Deerborn who was patting down a mound of dirt around a plant. He knew that if he was ever to go back to Maridia, going with Deerborn and Abril would be the most opportune chance to come his way.

"Deerborn," said Ethan, regarding his father as he did. "I want to go back to Maridia with you."

Deerborn looked up from his work. "What would you do that for? This is your home. Your family is here."

Deerborn looked at Amory.

"My father already knows my intentions," said Ethan.

"And how do you feel about this, Amory?" asked Deerborn.

"His mother and I are confident in his ability to choose his own path," said Amory, a smile on his face. A touch of sadness in his eyes subtly betrayed his smile.

"Well...we have just gotten here and would like to get to know your land better before we head south again," said

Deerborn. "I suppose it will be fine with us, if your parents are in agreement."

Ethan smiled. He couldn't hide his jubilation.

"Do you want to go to university in Maridia then?" asked Deerborn somberly.

"I was planning on it," said Ethan, halting in his work. "Why? Is something wrong? Jukes told me I could come back to study..."

"No, it's not that," interrupted Deerborn. "Rector Osric has been acting... a bit off lately."

"Really? How so?" asked Ethan.

"It's hard to put a finger on it. Come to think of it, he started acting kind of peculiar not long after I returned," Deerborn replied.

"*I* thought he was peculiar when I met him," laughed Ethan.

"Yes," answered Deerborn, with a discerning glare. "But it's different now. Been keeping to himself, he has. In fact, the only one who's seen him as of late, other than the students, of course, has been Alaric."

"What has Jukes said about the Rector's behavior?"

"Well, that's as queer as any other part of it," stated Deerborn. "Jukes is pretending like the Rector is fine."

"Do you think he just hasn't noticed a change in Osric?" asked Ethan.

"I'll say this-- if he hasn't noticed, then something's a bit off with the Overseer, too. At any rate, I just thought you should know about it before you commit to leaving your family behind."

"Um, thanks," said Ethan. But his mind was already made up.

* * *

Deerborn and Abril spent their short time in Glæm basking in the warmth of the close-knit Lambent family. Neither of them had living family in Maridia, so they looked on their time in Luminae with considerable fondness. The couple met all those families who were closest to the Lambents and found community in them, as well.

Deerborn had a splendid time one particular afternoon visiting with Mr. Taubs. The Maridian was amazed at the size of Taubs' farm, having come from a mountain town that lacked wide open spaces such as Glæm had to offer. Taubs gave Deerborn an extensive tour of his barns and their many departments: the Milkery, the Buttery, the Cheesery, and so on. Deerborn was most impressed at the size of Taubs' Lake. He had never seen any body of water over the size of a pond in the forest. All in all, Mr. Taubs and Deerborn became the best of acquaintances that day. Mr. Taubs spoke highly of the Captain of the Maridian Guard for years to come.

Abril spent her days being pampered by the Lambent women like a member of the family. Abril often expressed how she longed to have friends in Maridia such as she found in Eisley, Evangeline and Jaine. Though, the latter appeared ill at ease about something. When questioned by Eisley, Jaine donned an apprehensive smile and said, "I'm fine dear, I'm fine." Eisley knew better, though. Whatever was bothering her grandmother had something to do with the coming of their guests. Despite her concerned look, Jaine remained very hospitable towards Deerborn and Abril.

Even Poudis was having a splendid time. Living in a close-quartered, mountaintop citadel doesn't lend to as much running and playing as D'munes are known to enjoy. Poudis appeared to relish in the freedom of the fields, playing with (or rather annoying) Lewis and Lucy and all the other livestock. On one certain day, Galby the goat had had enough of Poudis' fidgety ways, and while the D'mune was running between his legs, the goat kicked Poudis and sent him sailing over the fence. Eisley and Abril heard the D'mune yelp and ran to the window just in time to see the poor creature skid across the yard. They ran to check on him, but he seemed unscathed, save his pride (which had suffered greatly). For a few days Poudis kept to the house, but before long he was back to his tiny gallivanting ways.

Ethan and Eisley's grandparents from Ilona, Charston and Noemi Hale, came to visit after receiving word, by post, that Ethan would soon be leaving. Noemi fell right in with the going-ons of the rest of the ladies. Charston found quite an associate in Deerborn as they spent hours on end discussing the Glæmian art of sword-smithing.

Weeks passed, yet Jaine's sullen attitude remained. Eisley began to really worry about her grandmother. Jaine was not one to wear her feelings on her sleeves like she had recently. One morning, while running up Woodline Road with her brother, Eisley came to an abrupt stop, a look of concern on her face.

"You okay?" asked Ethan returning to his sister's side.

"Have you noticed Grandma Jaine acting... I don't know, kind of peculiar?"

"Um...no, I don't think so," replied Ethan, trying to recall anything out of the ordinary. "Why? Has she?"

Moving closer to Ethan as if to discuss the matter more privately, Eisley whispered, "Yes, actually. She has seemed so sad and...distant lately. I think it started about the time that Deerborn and Abril got here."

"I haven't spent much time with her recently," said Ethan, ashamedly. "I'll be on the lookout for anything out of the ordinary. Though I can't imagine what Deerborn and Abril being here would have to do with it."

"Neither can I," said Eisley beginning to run again. Ethan came behind.

In the days that followed Ethan did notice a difference in his grandmother, just as Eisley had said. He decided to go and see Grandpa Emmett about the matter. Ethan found Emmett on a ladder against the side of his cottage re-mudding the stones high above his head.

"Grandpa!" said Ethan a bit louder than he'd meant to, startling the old man in the process. Emmett slipped, wrapping himself fast to the upper rungs, but his tools and the bucket of mud that had been resting on the top of the ladder tumbled to the ground. Finding his footing he said, "Boy I oughta...hmph...son, don't ya know better than to yell at someone on a ladder... especially when he's old and senile!"

"You're not senile, Grandpa," said Ethan trying hard to repress a laugh. "Sorry."

"It's okay, it's okay," said Emmett descending to the ground and pushing his white hair off his forehead. "What can I do for ya this fine day?"

"Well," began Ethan, "Eisley and I are worried about Grandma. She's been acting a bit odd lately."

"That she has, that she has," said Emmett trailing off into thought as he bent to retrieve his tools from the ground. Eisley was right. There was something wrong.

Ethan reached down and picked up the bucket that had landed upside down in the grass. Mud sloshed out covering his hands.

"Why don't we go inside and get you cleaned up, young man?" said Emmett.

Together they walked inside. Cleaning himself in the kitchen sink, Ethan peered over at his grandfather who had taken a seat at their small wooden table.

"So, worried 'bout your grandma, are ya?"

Ethan nodded.

"Good lad," said Emmett.

"Well, actually, Eisley noticed it first," said Ethan.

"Ah, I see," said Emmett. "Truth be told, she's upset that yer going off to Maridia."

"What? Why?" asked Ethan.

"Do you remember that heart to heart we had in the forest last year? When you and Eisley were leavin'?"

Ethan nodded, again.

"Remember how I told ya that yer Grandmother was from Farthenly?"

"Yeah."

"Well, what I didn't say then was that a long time ago, before yer Grandma was even born, Maridia attacked Farthenly and brought that little village to its knees."

Ethan understood now.

"But, Deerborn told me that Maridia released Farthenly from their control," said Ethan.

"Did he now? So you already knew?"

"Well, I'd forgotten, to be honest," said Ethan. "But Deerborn mentioned it on our trip to Gloam."

"Deerborn's right. Maridia finally let Jaine's home go back to their old way of doin' things. But they remained afraid of Maridia right up to yer grandma's time."

"So that's it?" asked Ethan.

"That's it," replied Emmett. "She's afraid that they might change you."

Ethan walked home pondering he and his grandpa's talk. Did his grandmother actually believe that Maridia could change him? He wasn't even sure what that meant. He liked the Maridians. He didn't feel like they were any different than himself except that they didn't know their Creator. But as Ethan had recently discovered, knowing the Light didn't automatically make you a good person. "You still have to work at doing the right thing," his father often said to him. Ethan thought there were lots of Glæmians that still had a big job before them. Not that *he* was perfect. But *he* had been through Gloam. *He'd* stared death in the face and come out on the other side believing in the Light. How then could Maridia change him?

Chapter Seven
A Parting of Ways

Ethan was soon to depart from Luminae, much like he had nearly a year before. But this time he'd go without Eisley. On their last adventure, it had comforted Ethan to know his sister was with him, making the journey to Gloam less lonely than it might have been without her by his side. But now, the thought of parting from Eisley brought on a feeling that he'd never experienced in his life. It was a type of trepidation that he'd not even felt when left, by himself, to the whims of the darkness. The split was inevitable: Ethan and Eisley were being led in different directions now-- him back to Maridia, and her back to Gloam. He didn't know how his sister was going to break the news to their parents that she would soon be leaving, too, and, as of yet, Eisley remained silent about her plans. He wondered when he and his sister's paths would cross again.

For days preceding his departure, Evangeline was teary-eyed. He didn't like seeing his mother cry. She'd told him that she was fine and that this was something every mother had to deal with at some point, but it didn't make it any easier on him. Ethan spent most evenings with his father and grandfather peering through an old rust-worn star-glass. As they studied the surfaces of the Brother Moons, Amory and Emmett poured practical advice of all sorts into Ethan. Later,

Ethan would remember these nights with much affection. He'd also taken the time to discuss his grandmother's uneasiness with her. Ethan tried to reassure her that he wouldn't let the people of Maridia change him or his beliefs. But Jaine said that it wasn't the people she was worried about; rather, it was an elusive foreboding that she couldn't explain. The time spent with his sister was the most bitter-sweet of all. They didn't say much, as each would get too emotional, so they just sat together, both enjoying the company of the other.

On the night before Ethan was to leave, he packed up his belongings. Looking around his life-long home, he gathered things that would be useful to him on his trip. The young man thought of bringing along Riley's Lantern, which stood proudly on the fireplace mantel in the sitting room. But he decided to leave it behind this time. After all, night had been dispelled from Gloam and the lantern would be rendered useless, even in Maridia. If occasion did call for the need of light, Ethan now glowed in the presence of complete darkness-- a thought that made him chuckle. Entering his room, he rolled up the unfinished map on his desk. He decided he was going to continue working on the map of Gloam while in Maridia. He wanted to present the map and his *Chronicle of Gloam's History and Culture,* as he'd named it, to Rector Osric. Ethan reached above his bed and removed a sword from the wall. It was the sword that Grandpa Charston had made him a few summers past. Ethan remembered how he'd wished he'd taken the sword on the last trip into Luminae Forest. He considered its weight and balance. He still had *Geong on Boud*, the sword that Deerborn had given him, yet his sister had lost its twin in the standoff against the Watchers. He thought his grandfather's sword suited him more, which made sense considering that it had been forged solely for him. This gave Ethan an idea-- he went next door to Eisley's room where he heard her singing through the crack in the door. He hated to interrupt her because she sang so beautifully. Ethan leaned against the wall in the hallway and listened. She was singing one of their father's songs called, *The Morning Song*. This is what she sang:

Open your eyes, oh Rosy Dawn,

And stretch your fingers to the sky,

The night will come before you know,

Don't let the day pass you by,

It's a new morn like those before,

Much to be done and ways to grow,

When the twilight tucks you in,

What work and toil is there to show?

Once she'd finished, Ethan wiped an expected tear away from his eye and then entered his sister's room bearing a gift.

"Hey, Eisley."

"Oh, hey," said Eisley. She saw that Ethan was holding *Geong on Boud.* "What are you doing with that?"

"I'm giving it to you," said Ethan, holding out the sheathed weapon.

Eisley reached for it. "Why?" she asked.

"Well, because you lost yours... and I still have the one Grandpa made for me."

"You haven't learned to fight with that type of sword though," said Eisley. It was true, Charston made swords in the old fashion. The ones he forged resembled the type of blade Deerborn wielded.

"I'll be living with Deerborn. He can teach me."

Eisley hugged her brother. "I love you," she said.

Ethan just nodded, holding back more tears.

"I know things are hard now, I mean here in Luminae," said Eisley, "But they'll get better. You'll see."

"You have Father's optimism," laughed Ethan. "You know that I'm not running away from the issue with Canis."

"Yes, I know."

"It's just time for me to go."

"I know that too."

* * *

The day arrived for Ethan, Deerborn, Abril, and Poudis to return to Maridia. The Lambents, the Hales, Canis, and Mr. Taubs gathered around to wish the company safe travel.

Eisley hugged Deerborn and Abril: they had become so dear to her. She'd wanted to tell them she'd visit soon, but in truth Eisley didn't know what her future held. Even in the newly found light, Gloam would surely be a dangerous place, especially if Watchers were still on the loose. Poudis got in on the goodbyes, leaping up into Eisley's arms to give her quite a messy face bath. Eisley squeezed the D'mune and spoke to it in a senseless tongue.

Ethan said his goodbyes one by one, first hugging and kissing his mother. He stood eye to eye with her, now.

"Be careful, my boy," said Evangeline.

"I will, Mama."

Then his father pulled him close and embraced him saying, "Remember who you are, son...a Lambent and a child of the Light."

Ethan hugged his father, nodding as he did.

Next he said his goodbyes to his grandparents. Emmett told Ethan that he wouldn't be following him this time, and they both laughed. But his smile faded when he saw Grandma Jaine's forlorn expression.

"Heed your father's words Ethan. Remember to whom you belong."

Whatever words Ethan had been planning to say got stuck in his throat at his grandmother's words.

"Everything will be fine Grandma," was all he could manage, still not understanding Jaine's fear. Her words left him feeling as apprehensive as she looked.

Charston and Noemi wrapped their arms around Ethan. Noemi kissed his cheek and Charston said, "Deerborn tells me that you might be able to apprentice with Maridia's blacksmith. You'd make your old grandpa proud if you did."

Ethan smiled, less at his grandfather's words and more at the bond his grandpa had formed with Deerborn.

Then he gave a very cordial handshake to Mr. Taubs who tussled Ethan's hair, nudging him on down the line of well-wishers.

Reaching Canis, Ethan embraced him like he would a brother and whispered, "Take care of my sister in Gloam."

Canis nodded resolutely. Only they knew of Eisley's plan to return to Canis' home.

Finally, he reached his sister. Eisley was pushing the grass around with one of her feet, trying to occupy her thoughts with something that wasn't sad. She stopped and looked up tearfully into Ethan's eyes. Over the winter and spring he'd grown taller than she, which was strange for them both since they'd always been the same height. He laid his hand upon her shoulder, nodded and smiled, tearfully. Then he took hold of Eisley, lifting her from the ground slightly.

"Be careful in Gloam, Eisley girl," Ethan whispered. "Stay by Canis' side."

"I will," cried Eisley as her brother set her back down.

At last, the trio and the D'mune headed towards the wood. When they got to the tree line the company turned (except for Poudis, of course, who had already galloped off into the forest.) Ethan gave one last wave that was returned by the long line of onlookers. Then they slipped into the shadows of Luminae Forest.

Chapter Eight
Something Always Goes Wrong in the Wood

Ethan and company traveled through the forest all day, passing many familiar landmarks-- Noodle Creek, Stepping Stone and even the Awakening clearing where the twins began their last journey. The trio made light conversation as they traversed over hill and hollow, occasionally cutting paths through the undergrowth. Spirits were high when the company decided to make camp for the night. Deerborn and Abril set up the tents while Ethan and Poudis gathered firewood. Actually, Ethan gathered firewood alone. Poudis did little more than try to snatch the wood from Ethan's hands, apparently thinking the chore more of a game. Soon there was a modest fire crackling. Abril prepared a hardy stew that they all ate to their contentment. Afterwards, they sat quietly around the campfire listening to the sounds of the forest. The wind rustled the changing leaves high above, sending sporadic showers of yellow, orange and red in their direction. The creaking of the branches and rustling of the leaves seemed to join in sacred melody with one another-- long sung yet never understood by human ears.

"Listen," said Abril, "it sounds as though the trees are serenading us."

"Aye, love," said Deerborn, "the forest is a place of magic, is it not?"

Ethan was reminded of the wildlife's chorus that often rose up when the Magic Lantern was lit. This time it was the trees' turn to lead the ancient song. "It's a place of adventure, too," smiled Ethan, lost in his memories.

"That it is. That it is," said Deerborn. "Which reminds me of something an old Maridian storyteller once wrote-- that forests are the places where one should expect adventures."

"I agree," said Ethan. "Who's the storyteller?"

"Dòmhnall," said Deerborn. "His name was Dòmhnall."

"Was he a farmer... no, a teacher I think, right?" said Abril.

"He was both," said Deerborn.

"What are his stories like?" asked Ethan.

"They are fantastical tales of lore," said Deerborn. "He used to be a favorite among the youth of Maridia."

"He used to be?" asked Ethan. "Why is he not now?"

"Stories of that nature are... frowned upon in Maridia these days," answered Abril.

"Really? Why?"

"Years ago, when Osric became the Rector of the university, he began a campaign to shelve the stories of lore and made a push to focus on topics that were of a more 'factual' nature, as he called them."

"Does anyone still read the old tales?"

"Most don't. It is an unpopular thing to do, so most don't."

"That is so strange."

"Indeed," said Deerborn, "and like I told you before, he's been even more unusual as of late."

"I didn't realize that Rector Osric had that kind of authority in Mari..."

Ethan was interrupted by Poudis who had sprung up from his slumber in a fit of growling.

"What's wrong, boy? Did you hear something?" asked Deerborn.

"*NURRRR PLLLET*," came a foreign sound from the nearby trees.

"What was that?" asked Ethan.

"Quiet," whispered Deerborn getting to his feet. He was focusing intently on the shadowy trees just beyond the campsite. Ethan stood as well. Poudis was shaking with alertness. Abril reached down and picked up the D'mune to calm him.

"*NURRRR PLLLET*," came the sound, much closer this time.

"There it is again," said Ethan.

Suddenly, the forest erupted in a rising and falling ensemble of *NURRRR PLLLET, NURRRR PLLLET, NURRRR PLLLET, NURRRR PLLLET, NURRRR PLLLET, NURRRR PLLLET, NURRRR PLLLET, NURRRR PLLLET.*

"Iver, what is that?" asked Abril.

"I'm not sure, Love," answered Deerborn.

Ethan was confused. Had Abril just called Deerborn-- Iver?

"Arm yourself, Ethan."

Deerborn's face creased with concern. The last time Ethan had seen his friend like this was in Gloam when the Captain was taken hostage. Ethan ran to his tent and returned with his sword. Deerborn now brandished his weapon as well.

The strange calls continued on, moving ever closer.

NURRRR PLLLET, NURRRR PLLLET, NURRRR PLLLET, NURRRR PLLLET, NURRRR PLLLET, NURRRR PLLLET, NURRRR PLLLET, NURRRR PLLLET.

Suddenly, two streams of a purplish substance shot out of the trees from somewhere high above, knocking the sword from Ethan's grasp. Ethan hurriedly bent to pick up his weapon and another stream of purple hit the sword, holding it fast to the ground. Then, tiny, white, creatures began to descend from the heights of the tree branches. So vast were their numbers that the brown tree trunks appeared to be turning white. Poudis leapt from Abril's arms and charged at the grotesque beings.

"Come back here you infernal D'mune!" shouted Deerborn. But it was too late- a stream of the purple sludge shot from the mouth of one the closest beasts and Poudis moved no more.

Deerborn ran to the fallen D'mune and tried to pull him loose from the ground. The hardened gunk wouldn't budge. The man rose and in a fit of rage ran headlong into the midst of the foe. The tiny imps began to climb upon one another rising up to tower above the Deerborn. Then they assaulted him with their foul spray. He desperately parried the incoming sludge for a few hopeful moments, but then the little creatures, having made a living blockade, began to overtake the man by sheer numbers alone. He flourished his sword fearlessly at the squirming wall before him. Wherever his sword struck, a few of the little devils would tumble to the ground, leaving a momentary hole in their rampart that was quickly filled by the seemingly never-ending supply of their ranks. Then, like one of the massive waves on the shores of Glæm, the wall crashed down upon Deerborn. He could no longer be seen amongst the scurrying commotion.

Abril screamed. Ethan looked on in disbelief. Coming to his senses, he grabbed Abril's hand, shouting, "We have to run!" He pulled her away. Seconds later, Ethan was hit hard from behind by something wet and he tumbled to the ground. He saw the creatures up close for the first time as they used their purple spray to hold him to the ground. Their faces were toad-like, their bodies more humanoid, standing upright. The hands and feet were webbed and at the end of each appendage was a tiny suction cup. From the corner of his eye, Ethan could see the monsters clamoring over a figure lying next to him. As his vision went purple, Ethan was sure they'd gotten Abril, as well, and then he fell unconscious.

The next thing Ethan knew, there was a small tongue lapping his eyes and nose. He couldn't move but now he could see. There was a D'mune on his chest, but it wasn't Poudis. This one was slightly larger and hairier than

Deerborn's pet. The D'mune hopped off Ethan's chest and began to lick at Ethan's hands, still held at his sides. In the distance, Ethan saw something that he could hardly comprehend and once realized he could barely believe. In the hollow before him there raged the strangest of battles ever recorded by the human mind-- the scary white creatures were fighting a large pack of D'munes! The latter was clearly outnumbered yet they held their ground. By the looks of it, the devils were a food for the D'munes. Even though the imps were equal in size, the D'munes' were making quick work of them: one bite would devour their top halves and a second would finish them off. There was no chewing to speak of.

Ethan could tell that his hand, the one the D'mune had been licking, was free now. The animal began licking at his other hand. Apparently, the D'munes saliva could break down the toxic compound of the little creatures. The D'mune finally got Ethan's other hand loose, which gave him enough leverage to wiggle his way up and out of his purple cocoon. Ethan bent to pet his savior in admiration, scanning the scene for signs of Deerborn and Abril. He found Deerborn aiding the D'munes in their fight, hacking and slashing at the imps around his ankles. As his sword made contact with the monsters they were sent flying this way and that, releasing their devilish little howls as they were lobbed away. The scene was a bit comical, as serious as the situation really was. Ethan heard a commotion behind him and found a few D'munes working fervently on Abril's bindings. Abril was unconscious. He noticed that the entirety of her face was covered which meant that she might have been without air for sometime. Running to her side, Ethan began to tear at the cocoon with all his might. He managed to break the purple fetter free from her mouth. To the young man's great relief, Abril drew in a long, life-giving breath. Soon, she was completely free.

In the time that Ethan had been focused on Abril, Deerborn and the army of D'munes had turned the tide and the imps were now on the run, sending *NURRRR PLLLET*'s into the air as they fled.

Deerborn watched the retreat briefly and then found his wife standing on the hillside with Ethan. He ran to meet her and took her up in his arms with such an affectionate embrace that Ethan turned away in embarrassment.

"Are you alright, my dear?" asked the war weary soldier.

"I... I think so," answered Abril. "Ethan, helped the D'munes to free me."

"Thank you, Ethan. Yet again, I owe you what can never be repaid," said Deerborn.

Chapter Nine

A Noticeable Decline

While the trio recuperated from the attack, Deerborn explained to the others what had happened after they'd been bound. He shared that his head had been left exposed so he'd watched helplessly as the mass of imps left him and moved to take down Ethan and Abril. At the same time, Poudis had awoken to find himself pinned to the ground. He began to yelp and howl. Soon after, Deerborn heard nearing movement in the forest and he feared that the creatures had reinforcements on the way. He thought better of it, though, when the devils stopped binding up Abril and began to move away from the near noise. Then a surge of D'munes burst through the bramble having come to the aid of the beckoning Poudis. A few began to free Poudis from his purple trappings while the others engaged the imps. When Poudis was freed he, and those who had helped release him, freed Deerborn. Deerborn made certain that some of the D'munes were releasing Abril and Ethan and he joined in the fight.

Now they all sat next to their tents much like they had before the attack, but with a few more guests gathered around the fire. Upwards of thirty D'munes were standing guard around the travelers. It was undoubtedly the oddest thing any of them had ever witnessed, which meant a great deal, two of them having traversed the land of Gloam. Because of their furry-guard the trio felt much safer. Not a single "*NURRRR PLLLET*" was anywhere to be heard.

Abril looked a little worse for the wear. Ethan hoped that her glassy gaze was nothing more than exhaustion. The next day, however, Abril looked considerably worse than the previous night. Deerborn noticed the change, too, and was questioning her much like a physician might his patient. Abril answered that her limbs felt slightly numb and she couldn't concentrate on anything for more than a few seconds at a time. She had dark circles beneath her eyes and her skin bore a clammy pallor about it. Deerborn asked Ethan how he was fairing, trying to gauge a comparison with his wife. But Ethan felt just fine all things considered.

The company began their trek towards Maridia surrounded by their newly acquired escort. The D'munes carried themselves nobly. They seemed to have a keen look of awareness in their eyes, which made Ethan think they might spark up a conversation with their charge at any moment. Much to Ethan's disappointment, they did not.

The going was slow because Abril was having a hard time moving along. But move along they did and before long they reached the beginnings of what should have been the mountain range. The company had come upon a giant clearing and Ethan was certain that this had been the way he and Eisley had come last time. Breaching the tree-line, Ethan found what Deerborn and Abril had already discovered on their trip to Luminae. Before him was a gaping hole where once there had stood a mountain. Looking over the sheer edge, Ethan found the bottom some few hundred feet below. He hadn't realized how much of the Ancients had rested beneath the surface.

Skirting the edge of the precipice Ethan saw several caverns that had been burrowed into the sides of the main hole. After passing a few more Ancient nesting holes the company began to hear the eerie call of their assailants again. This time, however, it was coming from the depths of the caverns. Apparently this is where the creatures came from. Perhaps they'd been drawn out of the deep darkness of the underworld by the uprooting of the Ancients, ascending to the surface after many lifetimes spent below. It would have most certainly accounted for their pale hides. Looking around at their D'mune caravan, Ethan realized that these majestic little animals must have been displaced from their homes much the same way as the cave imps had, for according to Deerborn, Poudis and his kind had lived on the backs of the Ancients. More than anything, these musings did much to ease Ethan's mind concerning the fact that he'd not run into any such creatures on his first journey. When the mountains moved it had obviously stirred up the imps, nesting below, in much the same way as Canis had stirred up the citizens of Luminae.

Ethan, Deerborn and Abril camped one last night on their journey. On the morning of the third day, they saw a glorious sight: the Western Lookout rose high into the sky nearly blotting out the sun above. Their arrival couldn't have been more opportune because Abril's health had worsened. Deerborn began to call up the hillside to his watchman who descended the massive hillock with ease. The men stood, mouths agape, looking at the surrounding D'mune army while Deerborn explained what had happened. A wagon was brought around to get Abril to Maridia's healer as quickly as possible.

It wasn't long before the travelers were loaded up on the wagon and preparing to depart towards the mountain-top citadel. Ethan couldn't help but feel a bit of nostalgia being back on the very same wagon that had borne him, shackled, to Maridia almost a year earlier. He smiled. As the horse drawn company left the Western Lookout behind, they watched the army of D'munes disappear northward into the forest.

Chapter Ten
The City on the Hill

Ethan napped on the ride from the Western Lookout to Maridia. He woke to the sound of the wagon being loaded on the giant hillside lift. Raising his head over the side of the cart, he watched the lift as it rumbled upwards. Gathering his belongings, Ethan waited in anticipation to see the city's gates. He was glad to be back. The wagon made its way off the platform and up the road.

"You look excited," mustered the man whose mind was clearly on his wife's welfare. Abril's head lay in Deerborn's lap and he was running his fingers through her hair.

"I'm glad to be here again. But I wish it wasn't under these circumstances." He looked sympathetically toward Abril.

"Aye," said Deerborn. "I wish that, as well."

"So... Iver?" asked Ethan.

"Ah, you heard Abril say my given name, did you?"

Ethan smiled and nodded.

"She's the only one who calls me that and only when she's worried," said Deerborn, brushing the back of his fingers across Abril's cheek. The man's eyes had become pools of sadness over the course of the day.

"Will the Healer be able to figure out what's wrong with her?" asked Ethan.

"I can't say for sure. If she was poisoned by those little demons, as I believe she was, then our healer may not have a cure."

"What were those things?" Ethan asked.

"I'm not exactly sure. But I recall something like them in the old stories I told you about."

"Those are just stories, though, aren't they?"

"Are they? Perhaps there is some truth to those tales."

"Maybe there is. The Boy of Legend, from Glæmian tales turned out to be real."

"That he did. That he did," reflected Deerborn.

"You should go to the library and ask Naava about the imps. I've been told that she knows about every book on every shelf there. If that's true, she might be able to find the creature in the old stories."

"That is quite an idea, Ethan. Dòmhnall might have even written about a cure for their poison."

Soon they reached the gateway. Soldiers pulled the iron gates open, saluting Deerborn as he passed. Deerborn directed the driver toward the Healer's dwelling place. As they approached, a sizable crowd, diverted from their daily business, began to form around the wagon. Hearing the commotion, the Healer came out and assessed the scene. He listened intently to Deerborn's account of the attack. Deerborn carried his limp wife into the Healer's home, to an empty examination table and the old physician immediately began to examine Abril.

The door burst open, startling Ethan. The Overseer and his daughter rushed in. For the briefest of moments Ethan and Delia locked eyes and just as quickly looked away from each other. Ethan wasn't sure what to feel in that moment being so caught up in Deerborn's sorrow. Seeing Delia for the first time in long while suddenly birthed emotions of a different sort in his mind. His head was a whirlwind of confusion.

"Oh my, what's happened, Deerborn?" asked Jukes.

"We were attacked in the forest," answered Deerborn, never taking his eyes off Abril.

"By whom?" asked the Overseer.

"You mean, by what?"

"I'm sorry, Deerborn, but I don't follow."

Deerborn finally looked at Jukes.

"We were attacked by an army of nasty little creatures, the likes of which I've never seen."

"What? What were they? Some sort of animal?"

"No, I don't think so. They were too intelligent to be animals."

"What then?" asked Jukes in bewilderment.

"I hesitate to answer that question...yet."

Deerborn watched in disappointment as the Healer encountered one road block after another in his attempted diagnosis of Abril's condition. After many trials the verdict remained inconclusive.

"I'm sorry but I have never seen these symptoms together," admitted the Healer. "I'm afraid I'm not sure how to treat her..."

"I'll return soon. Will you look after Abril while I'm gone?" asked Deerborn, moving quickly towards the door.

"I will do what I can, Deerborn," said the Healer.

The door slammed shut behind the Captain. Jukes turned to Ethan for further explanation. He began to recount the battle in the forest and how the D'munes had come to rescue them from the imps. The Overseer looked unconvinced of the truth of his story.

"Where did Deerborn rush off to?" asked Jukes.

"I think he went to the library. He wants to ask Naava about the creatures."

The Overseer's face suddenly flashed bright red. He left the Healer's home in much the same fashion that he'd entered it. Delia and Ethan followed, trailing closely behind the Overseer. They crossed the town, whose citizenry had already gone back to their previous business, though a feeling of curiosity still flitted in the air about the town. Going in the library, Ethan spotted Deerborn bent over a large leather-bound volume reading intently. From somewhere in the rear of the building the voice of old Miss Naava could be heard questioning Deerborn further about the creatures.

"Deerborn, surely you don't think you're going to find answers in those books," said Jukes, storming up next to him.

"This isn't the right type, Naava," shouted Deerborn, ignoring Jukes altogether. "They were much shorter and they weren't green. They were white."

"White, did'ya say? Hmm...did they make any noise?"

"Yes! NURPEL something or other."

"Ah, ha!" said Naava, triumphantly.

Seconds later the old hunched lady came scurrying up one of the side aisles carrying an even larger tome than the one sitting before Deerborn. Shooing Jukes and Delia out of the way, the old librarian dropped the big book on the long wooden table with resounding PLOP!

"Oh, fiddle sticks!" exclaimed the old lady. "I hate it when I drop a book like that. My old arms don't work like they use'ta." Looking up, Miss Naava found Ethan. Smiling widely she said, "Hey there Lambent boy! I heard'ya found the way out of that awful Gloam! One in a million chance. Though it does run in the family, huh, boy?"

"I suppose so," said Ethan, smiling to greet the old lady.

Before Deerborn opened the new book, Ethan got a good look at the title: *The Whimsical World Unknown* written by none other than Dòmhnall, the famous Maridian storyteller.

"Still got Earnest's journal young man?" asked Miss Naava.

"Yes, ma'am," said Ethan, tearing his thoughts away from the book. "It's at home with my family now."

"Hmm, that's a shame, I was hoping to see it again," said the old librarian. "These books'r kinda like friends to me. Yep, like old friends."

"Here it is!" shouted Deerborn, pointing at a page. "This is one of the little terrors right here!"

Naava sidled up next to Deerborn to get a better look at the small pale creature. "Uh huh, just as 'spected- Cave Imps.

Better known as Nurplets 'cause 'o the noise they make. Ran into some did'ya?"

"They ran into us is more like it," answered Ethan.

"Mighty peculiar," said Naava.

"You can't be serious, Deerborn," joined Jukes. "It must have been something else. Er, possibly an animal that looked similar. I implore you to see reason, man!"

"This-is-what-attacked-us," answered Deerborn tapping the picture with each word. He seemed to be growing angry by the Overseer's distrust in him.

Jukes' look was calculating. With a sigh of frustration he turned to leave.

"Osric won't be happy about this," mumbled the Overseer, as he walked away. Turning he bade Delia to follow him. She stared deeply into Ethan's eyes for one long moment then curtsied, turned, and followed her father out of the library.

"Can I take this book, Naava? I need to find out as much as I can about these...Nurplets."

"O'course ya can. Anything to help poor Abril."

Deerborn closed the book and a large plume of dust rose up from its long unread pages. Naava caught a mouthful of the dust and waddled off to her desk coughing. Together Ethan and Deerborn left the library with the slightest hope of finding a cure for Abril.

Chapter Eleven
Life's Complexities

Ethan had been invited to sup at the Overseer's home the day following his arrival. Now the young man sat across from Alaric and Delia Jukes who hadn't spoken a word since first welcoming Ethan into their home. The dull clanking of wooden utensils on wooden plates had been the only sound for a good portion of the meal. Ethan looked up from his roast and noticed Delia's eyes dart away from him. Jukes noticed, too, and grunted.

"I'm glad to hear Deerborn has moved Abril to their home," said Delia, relieving the awkward tension.

"Yeah, me, too," answered Ethan, hoping this had diverted the Overseer's thoughts. The last time Ethan had seen the Jukes' family was when he'd kissed Delia on the cheek in front of her father. He hadn't expected the reunion to go quite like it was at present.

"Um...yes," began Jukes half-mindedly. "The Healer stopped by today and told us that Abril's condition hadn't changed. I think it was wise of Deerborn to move his wife to their home. She'll do much better in her own surroundings."

"You think so?" asked Ethan.

"Well, the least we can do is *hope* so. Right?" said Jukes.

"Yes. We can hope," answered Delia.

"Why don't you believe Deerborn?" asked Ethan, getting to the subject that was really on his mind.

"Now, really...I wish to not have such nonsensical conversation over dinner," replied Jukes. "It's not good for the digestion process."

Out of respect for his host, Ethan complied. He could see that he'd really hit a sore spot.

"There are other matters, more important matters, we need to discuss," said the Overseer, trying to act more cheerful with the sudden change of topic. "I have promised you an education, haven't I?"

"Yes, sir, you did," replied Ethan.

"Though I'm ashamed to admit it, I never thought I'd have to keep that promise. What, with you going off into Gloam..."

"Father!" interrupted Delia.

"But, never mind that now. You're here and you're safe and I'm a man of my word. Tomorrow I'll take you to see Rector Osric and to enroll in the university."

"Thank you, sir," answered Ethan, still pondering the Overseer's comments.

"Ah...you thank me now but we'll see how grateful you are after your meeting with the Rector. He's not particularly fond of taking in new students after the course of study has begun for the year."

Ethan looked down at his food.

"Though for you I think he'll make an exception. As you know, he's always wanted to teach a Glæmian."

"Why? I wonder," asked Delia.

Jukes considered his daughter's question for a moment before answering, "He probably wants to see what makes the Glæmians...tick."

Ethan's head shot up.

"Now, now. Don't look so worried, my boy. I'm only joking. I don't rightly know why Osric would be so interested in the Glæmians. Perhaps he's just curious about your customs, your beliefs."

"I'd be glad to share them," said Ethan, trying to hide his apprehension.

"I'm sure of it," answered Jukes. "That aside, there is one other matter to discuss. While there is no need to compensate me or the school for your education, you will have need for income. For instance, you will need to pay for your living quarters. Where will you be staying, by the by?"

"Deerborn and Abril have offered their spare room to me, um... free of charge," answered Ethan.

"Good, good," answered Jukes exchanging glances with Delia. "Be that as it may, you will still be in need of money to purchase things as you need them. As such, I have taken the liberty of acquiring work for you."

"You did? Where?"

"You will be working along side Mikael Temujin, the local blacksmith. I believe you've met him?"

"Yes, sir, I have."

"I hope I didn't overstep my bounds in this decision. Deerborn told me of your previous experience with smithing. You worked with your grandfather, I believe it was?"

"Yes, sir, I did. I appreciate your thoughtfulness," said Ethan. "I'll be happy to work with Mikael, if he needs me."

"Very well then," began Jukes, "meet me here at sun up and we'll see about enrolling you in school."

The Overseer rose from his place at the table, as did Delia and Ethan.

"I'm sorry, but we really must retire early tonight," said Jukes. "It has been a rather stressful day trying to maintain calm after Abril's um...mishap."

Ethan held his frustration. "Thank you for all of your hospitality," he said. "I'm really glad to be back." He risked a look at Delia. She smiled, shyly.

"Maridia is glad to have you back, my boy, I'm sure," said Jukes.

Ethan bid the Jukes family good evening and left their home. He walked out into the center of town and took a seat on the empty fountain that would never hold water because, as he now knew, the city was on the back of an Ancient and not a mountain. Or were they? It would have definitely accounted for the lack of water and the need for the lift; both a byproduct of being incapable of penetrating the surface of the mountain. Then again, the Ancient that Maridia sat upon hadn't left with the others and neither had the Eastern and Western Lookouts. Ethan thought the Ancients had remained because of the humans residing on them. But surely, some of the Maridians had questioned the stability of their home after the flight of the surrounding hills. In fact, this seemed just as fantastical and unbelievable as the Nurplets, if not more so. It isn't every day that one sees mountains take flight. Or had they seen them take flight? The Ancients had come to the Lambents' aid in Gloam during the lesser light so perhaps the Maridians had been asleep.

Ethan wondered why Jukes didn't believe Deerborn's account of the attack on Abril? It all seemed too odd. As did Jukes' comment about the Rector wanting to see what "makes the Glæmians tick." Deerborn did say that Rector Osric had been acting peculiar. What did it all mean? One thing was certain: there was more to Maridia than he'd known. Much the way he felt about Glæm. Why was everything so complex? Ethan longed for simplicity.

Ethan strolled back toward Deerborn's home, taking in the city night. Lamps were lit in many of the windows, yet the town was perfectly visible from the night sky alone. During his last visit, the magical clouds of Gloam had encroached on Maridia, blocking the Brother Moons' path through the night sky, making it much darker than Glæm. Now that the darkness had been subdued and the clouds wiped away, Maridia shown in the night just like Glæm. Several passersby nodded at Ethan as he walked. He recognized none of them but greeted them, just the same.

When Ethan arrived at the section of the citadel wall that was Deerborn's home, he noticed that most of the lights were out. Thinking the household asleep, Ethan entered quietly. There at the small kitchen table, Ethan found Deerborn passed out. He was snoring loudly. Ethan grinned. Deerborn was asleep on the book of lore that he'd been researching to find a cure for Abril. Taking a moment to inspect what Deerborn had been reading, Ethan read, aloud, the title on the page: "The Queen of the Nurplets." The rest of the page was blocked by Deerborn's bewhiskered face. He noted the page number for further inspection. Walking to the modest sitting area at the back of the room, Ethan heard a small whimper and turned to see Poudis at the top of the stairwell. Ethan guessed that the D'mune, having been by Abril's side since she'd been moved to her home, had come to inspect the new arrival. Satisfied that Ethan was not a trespasser, Poudis scuttled off toward Deerborn and Abril's room.

Plopping down in a chair, Ethan sat in silence, wondering how Deerborn was planning to help Abril. He was sure that the man would go to any length to help his wife. As Ethan began to nod off to sleep, his last conscious thought was that, he, too would do what he could to help her.

His face was concealed in shadow, behind the stream of sunlight...

Chapter Twelve
The Way to Knowledge

That night, Ethan dreamt that he was lying on his back, looking up at the stars. But something was out of place: the sky was too dark. There were no moons. The stars shown like never before and there were thousands of them, twinkling in and out in the great expanse above. Ethan felt a familiar sensation in his feet, an odd one to be lying on his back like he thought he was. He quickly realized that he was standing on ground. He wasn't looking at stars at all but rather at numerous sets of tiny eyes blinking in and out and illumined by himself in the darkness. In the midst of the eyes, another pair began to emerge...a larger pair. As the bulbous orbs drew closer, the tiny eyes scattered, climbing past the edges of Ethan's sight. The bigger eyes edged closer. Ethan began to tremble and then he heard a familiar voice calling out to him.

"Ethan," said the older voice. "Wake up young man!"

Ethan opened his eyes and gasped. Someone was in his face trying to shake him out of his slumber. Still caught between waking and sleeping, Ethan pushed away from the face. The chair he'd slept in tumbled over backwards CLACKING onto the floor. Somewhere above, Poudis started yelping.

"Good heavens... are you alright?" asked Alaric Jukes.

Deerborn chuckled.

"Yeah, I think so," said Ethan getting to his feet, examining the back of his head. "I hit my head, though."

"Well I should think you did," said Jukes. "You took quite a fall there."

"Yeah," laughed Ethan. "I was having a nightmare."

"Would you like some breakfast Ethan?" asked Deerborn, standing at the fireplace over a bubbling pot of porridge. The aroma hinted of blueberries.

The smell was welcoming and Ethan was hungry. Ethan nodded but Jukes interrupted saying, "I'm afraid he doesn't have time for breakfast now, Deerborn. Ethan slept late. I asked him to meet me at sun up, which has come and gone now. We have an appointment to keep with Rector Osric and we don't want him waiting any longer."

Ethan apologized for oversleeping. He couldn't even remember falling asleep, let alone upright in a chair. How he'd slept the night through in such an uncomfortable position was a mystery. But he had and there was a dull pain in his neck to prove it.

Ethan excused himself and ran upstairs to his room to freshen up. After splashing himself in the face with a basin-full of cold water and changing his tunic he was ready to go. Leaving his room, he peeked in on Abril who was still unconscious on her bed. Her chest rose and fell at a steady rate. Ethan hoped this was a good sign. Poudis lifted his head from the far side of Abril, having sensed an intruder. Ethan waved at the D'mune then ran down stairs to join Jukes, much more alert now.

Ethan followed the Overseer to the university's grand entryway, inscribed in stone with the words: THE WAY TO KNOWLEDGE. Crossing under the looming proclamation, Ethan felt a surprising foreboding about his decision to study in Maridia. He'd been so intrigued by Maridian culture and philosophy at his last visit, yet, after his struggle with the darkness and embracing his Creator he'd become a different person. Knowledge was still important to him, of course, but at what cost? If the Rector had been the one to ban all literature considered to be folklorish in nature then how was the man going to respond to Ethan's changes? After all, he did shine in total darkness. He took shameful comfort in the fact that he wouldn't be glowing in Maridia now that Smarr had been stopped and the clouds were forced away. At least he'd appear to be like the Maridians. Though he'd recently told his sister otherwise, perhaps he'd only been running from his life in Luminae after all.

How many more of his beliefs would clash with those of the Rector? One of the last pieces of advice Ethan's father gave him before leaving was that there was only one truth in life and it flowed from the Creator. He'd said that elements of that truth could be found in many cultures throughout the world. But sometimes the truth was peppered with lies and misunderstandings. Amory warned his son that this might be the case in Maridia and Ethan knew his father was right. He already had many differing ideas about life, where the Maridians were concerned. Many of these difference were beginning to take shape in his mind as he walked down the echoing corridor toward Osric's office. Ethan resolved to stick with his choice, come what may. Grandpa Emmett had said, "What don't kill ya, will only make ya stronger." Ethan hoped his grandpa was right.

They arrived at the Rector's study to find the door open and the room empty.

"I feared this might happen," said Jukes.

"What?" asked Ethan.

"We're late. The Rector is already in class. But perhaps I can pull him away."

Ethan was instructed to take a seat in the Rector's office while Jukes went to search for the man. The Overseer returned promptly, having talked with Osric. Ethan was advised to wait for the Rector to come to him. Jukes, looking pleased with the situation, set off to do whatever it is that Overseers do all day, leaving Ethan to his thoughts.

The Rector's study was much darker than Ethan remembered from his last visit. One solitary window was set in the wall, high above the Rector's desk. A stream of light steadily coursed in from the window, passing over the Rector's chair, which sat in relative darkness. The light fell across the desktop and poured over onto Ethan's seat. There were two large bookcases situated on the wall to his right where, Ethan was sure, there had definitely been windows the last time. Maybe the Rector was in need of more shelves for his large collection of books, some of which were stacked in the corners behind his desk. Whatever the case, the missing windows made the room feel much more foreboding. On the wall behind him hung a giant painting. It was a rendering of Rector Osric, seated at his desk in the most austere of poses: chin held high, beard combed to a fine point, a book held tightly to his chest. The painting was so lifelike that had the Rector actually been sitting in his high-back chair, the painting would have looked more like a mirror facing the man. From the ceiling hung a large candle-laden chandelier that was covered in spindly wax stalactites, some hanging at least a foot from the ornate structure. The marble floor, the guest chairs, and even the edge of the Rectors desk were all speckled with candle droppings.

Ethan sat there in the dim study for what felt like several hours. He'd nodded off when he heard the booming voice of the Rector entering the room.

"Sleeping again, I see," said the Rector.

Ethan startled to life, sitting up straight in his chair.

"I'm...sorry, sir," answered Ethan.

"You should know that alertness and punctuality are matters not to be taken lightly within these walls."

"Yes, sir."

"If you aspire to join the ranks of the learned, you must act accordingly."

"Yes.."

"Further..." interrupted the Rector, "I am not accustomed to taking in students after courses have resumed."

Rector Osric sat down at his desk. His posture was slightly hunched. His face was concealed in shadow, behind the stream of sunlight that teamed with dust motes. The man still had the scholarly beard, though, now it was more gray than black. His hair-line had receded, exposing a pallid, moist forehead. His eyes were fierce and sunken, surrounded by dark circles. A frightening display to be sure and little of the man Ethan met the year before. Little of the man displayed in the painting behind him. The ghostly man remained silent for some time. He appeared to be deliberating about something.

"In your case," said the Rector finally, "I think I will make an exception." His face was oddly expressionless.

"Thank you," said Ethan forcing himself to smile.

"Naturally, you will have to be tested in order for us to ascertain your present knowledge base."

Ethan nodded.

"We will quiz you in the areas of arithmetic, grammar, literature, philosophy, both natural and metaphysical, and, of course, history. Though in the last two subjects, I think you will need special attention," said Osric with a knowing smirk breaking through his otherwise unemotional gaze.

Ethan understood his meaning, realizing that both his philosophies of life and his understanding of history would be drastically different than what the University of Maridia taught. Ethan was interested in learning the Maridian views of history. He'd been taught that everything was created by the Light, which set the course of history in motion-- a lesson he fully trusted. Maridian instructors would certainly teach differently.

"How old are you, Ethan?"

"Thirteen...almost fourteen."

"Thirteen...almost fourteen," repeated Osric, a hint of sarcasm in his voice. "Well, that is another matter entirely, then. You are years younger than our average student. That being said, it may be of little consequence. Dependent, of course, upon your test results."

The Rector stood and moved toward Ethan, motioning for him to rise, too. Placing a hand on Ethan's shoulder the unnerving man said, "I will see that you are tested at our earliest convenience. You should have a date no later than the end of this week."

The two left the study walking side by side toward the university's exit. By the light of the lanterns proudly hanging from their sconces on the walls of the immense corridor, Ethan saw, once more, the battle scene he'd studied on his previous visit. The carved relief reminded him of his family and he wondered what was happening back home. Had things gotten worse for Canis or had the whole situation finally died down? He longed to know.

Chapter Thirteen
Of Secret Meetings and Strategies

A few days passed with no word from the Rector about Ethan's exam date. Ethan spent most days in the library, skimming through Maridian history books or helping Deerborn take care of Abril. He hadn't so much as seen Delia since dining at her home. Ethan wondered if Jukes had been keeping her busy to keep them apart.

Ethan had also gone to talk with the blacksmith, Mikael Temujin. Mikael was a slender, young man who, as time revealed, was a rather quiet individual. He and Mikael discussed the particulars of Ethan's apprenticeship in his shop. Ethan was to earn a feorthing a day, which Mikael admitted was modest pay but considering that Ethan's room and board were taken care of, it would more than suffice. Mikael confessed that his smithy was easily run by one person and that he'd taken Ethan on as more of a favor to Deerborn and Jukes. Ethan didn't like the idea of being at the receiving end of someone's charity, if his help wasn't actually needed. But he respected Mikael for telling him the truth and said that he'd do whatever needed to be done and more in return for hiring him. He informed the young blacksmith of the things he already knew about smithing, impressing Mikael who, though conservative in expressing himself, showed great exuberance in listening to Ethan tell of Glæmian blacksmithing. Ethan learned that many of Grandpa Charston's techniques were similar to Mikael's, though the latter did have his own trade secrets. By the end of their meeting Ethan was actually excited to start learning some of these secret techniques.

Finally nearing the end of his first week in Maridia, Ethan received a letter from a school messenger, a young woman whom he believed to be a student. The letter was sealed with a dark red wax bearing a bold 'M,' for Maridia in the center. He sat down next to the fire, pulled the letter open and read.

Dear Ethan Lambent,

Your presence is hereby promptly requested tomorrow morning in the classroom of Professor J. Jury of Maridia University's History Department. Professor Jury will administer the entrance exam, which we have previously discussed.

R.O.

In the hours that followed, Ethan crammed for the test, trying his best to prove the Rector wrong. He wanted to excel in every area of the exam, and while he felt that he held an adequate knowledge of the other subjects, he was sure he needed more time to study history and philosophy. He was nervous being sent to the History Department, of all places, to take the test. Perhaps this had been part of a plan to intimidate him. Having been educated under the loving guidance of his mother and father, Ethan was unused to the anxieties that were now culminating within him. Maybe it had all been coincidence, maybe the Rector hadn't been trying to frighten him. Intentional or not, Ethan certainly was frightened. He was frightened by the Rector's intense look of disdain towards him. He was frightened by how his beliefs might be dissected in the presence of a class of students older than himself. There were many other anxieties coursing through him. Too many to speak off. It was all he could do hold them at bay.

Ethan sat by Abril's side in the quiet home studying. Abril was Ethan's only steady company, as Deerborn, seeming more busy than normal, had been coming in and going out all day long. Deerborn acted like he was preparing for something. Maybe he had a plan to help Abril now. Finally, feeling lonely and cooped up in the small home, Ethan closed the book he'd been studying, *Generations, A Precise Lineage of Maridian Overseers,* and went for a much needed walk in the fresh air.

Even outside, he felt claustrophobic. The walls of the city seemed to press in on him and he longed to gaze out over the expansive fields of north Luminae. Ethan decided to leave the city for a while and go for a walk to visit his ancestor's tomb; the grave of Earnest Lambent.

Nearing the gates, the Glæmian thought he saw someone out of the corner of his eye. He turned to see a relatively empty street. The closest thing to him was the fountain and beyond that only a few pedestrians going about their evening business. Passing through the gate he found that the guards were not at their posts. Two of them sat in the guard house eating their suppers. They would not have noticed him if he hadn't waved, but he did and they waved in return, expeditiously returning to their fare. When Ethan was almost out of sight of the gate he heard a scuffling behind him. He turned in time to see a shadow dart back inside the gate. Ethan ran back to the citadel entrance, feeling paranoid. Still there was no one there. Three guards shot Ethan an inquisitive look but didn't get up from their meal. It was possible that his eyes were playing tricks on him as they often did after hours spent with his nose in a book. Shrugging it off he took up his walk again, heading out toward the tombs. Minutes later he arrived at the massive stone crypt and circled around to the rear where Earnest Lambent was forever incased. When he rounded the corner someone was standing there. Ethan let out a cry.

"Shhh," said the cloaked figure, "It's just me."

Delia took off her hood.

"Wha...what are you doing here?" breathed Ethan, leaning against the mausoleum.

"I was sitting at my window looking out over the town and I saw you come out of Deerborn's. I decided to follow you. We really need to talk."

"How did you beat me here? I saw you behind me."

"I've lived here my whole life, Ethan," laughed Delia. "I know my way around better than you, I should think."

She grinned teasingly.

Ethan felt a wave of insecurity spill over him. It was the first time they'd spoken so many words since his return.

"Why are you sneaking around?" he said, more defensively than he meant to.

Delia's expression became uneasy. "My father doesn't want me around you."

"I thought so. But why?"

"I'm not sure. Father hasn't been very clear about the reason. He's meeting with Rector Osric and Deerborn right now and they asked not to be disturbed so I thought I'd risk meeting you."

"I wonder what they're meeting about?" asked Ethan.

"It seemed really important. I think it has to do with Abril," explained Delia. "You should know that I'm not in the habit of disobeying my father, but I had to speak with you privately."

"Well, here we are. What's going on?"

"Okay...well, father's been acting strange. He seems too concerned with keeping Rector Osric happy."

"Yeah, I noticed, is that not normal?"

"No!"

Ethan looked taken aback.

"I'm sorry for yelling. I'm just so frustrated with my father right now."

"It's okay."

"Then there's Osric. He seems sick or something."

"I thought so, too!" said Ethan.

"And in a very foul mood," added Delia.

"That, too," laughed Ethan.

"I don't know what's going on but we need to find out," said Delia.

"Deerborn seems to think that things started getting weird after he returned from Gloam," said Ethan. "But he can't swear to it."

"Yeah," said Delia. "I think he might be right. I thought it had more to do with your first visit to Maridia. Now that I think about it, though...father was acting normal up until Deerborn returned. Ethan, please be on the look out for anything else curious."

"Okay. I will. But...if Jukes doesn't want us to see each other, how will I report it?"

"I'll figure something out," answered Delia. "I've got to go now."

"Bye," said Ethan awkwardly.

"Good-bye, Ethan."

Delia looked inquisitively at Ethan for a moment as if wanting to say something else. Then the moment passes and she drew up her hood, brushed past Ethan, and slipped around the corner. Ethan stood alone at the crypt with only his thoughts to keep him company. His mind raced as he walked back to the city trying to make sense of the unfolding mystery that he somehow landed himself right in the middle of. It frustrated him to no end. At the gate he found Deerborn huddled in conversation with the guards. Deerborn spotted Ethan, excused himself from his conversation, and ran over to him.

"Ethan, I've been looking for you."

"Sorry, I was out at Earnest's gravesite."

"No harm done. Listen, I'm leaving in the morning. I think I've found a way to help my wife."

"Really! Can I help?"

"No, I'm afraid not, Ethan. You need to focus on your studies. The Rector tells me you have your exam in the morning."

"Yeah, but helping you is more important. Right?"

"You can help me by looking after the house. The Healer's wife has agreed to stay with Abril while I'm gone, but there will be plenty of chores that need doing."

"Can you at least tell me your plan?"

"I don't have time to explain right now. Maybe we can talk later."

"Let me help you Deerborn, please!"

"Ethan, what I am going to do is risky and it might place you in unnecessary danger. I can't let you go. Please understand. I have much to do before I leave. Maybe we will talk later."

Deerborn patted Ethan on the shoulder and headed back to the guard house.

Ethan's frustration reached new heights. He knew he could help but he needed to know what Deerborn was planning. Ethan remembered the page that Deerborn had fallen asleep on days before. Thinking the page might hint at Deerborn's plan, he ran back home to find Dòmhnall's book of lore.

Ethan flipped to the page and gasped at the picture. The queen of the cave imps was masterfully illustrated along the bottom of the page, right where Deerborn had been lying on the book. With a shutter Ethan recognized the pale illumined eyes. They were the same eyes that Ethan had seen in his dream earlier that week. According to the surrounding text, if a human ingested the purple saliva of the Nurplet it would cause an unending sleep; one, in which all the organs remained in a state of dormancy. Dòmhnall explained that there was only one antidote for the poison: the blood of the Nurplet Queen.

Ethan closed the book and exhaled deeply. Deerborn planned to look for the queen. He would need help if his plan was to enter the caves. Ethan could light the way. He'd have to follow Deerborn if he wanted to help him, though. Then another thought came to him. Ethan would have to miss the exam. He shuddered at the thought of upsetting Rector Osric further, but he had no choice. Abril was far more important.

Chapter Fourteen
Clandestine Measures

Ethan arose before sun up. He'd stayed up late into the night deciding what he would do and the time had come to execute his plan. Ethan dressed and prepared a carryall of extra clothes and food, such as would last on the journey. He donned a brown cloak that had been given to him a few years prior. It was shorter than he'd remembered, but it would have to do. He strapped his short sword to his back, threw on the carryall and left his room in silence. Deerborn's bedroom door was cracked and the voice of Deerborn floated from the room. He was talking to his wife assuring her that upon his return he'd have a cure for her. Heart aching, Ethan tiptoed down the stairs hoping not to wake Poudis. He succeeded and crept silently out of the house. Skirting the perimeter of the town by the pale moonlight, Ethan felt excitement building. The trick was going to be getting through the closed gate. As Ethan neared the gate he saw that it had already been opened, perhaps in preparation for Deerborn's early departure. Now his only obstacle would be the guards. One stood inside the guard house and the other stood outside the gate. Sneaking up behind a stack of crates, Ethan called out in a deep voice to the guard beyond the gate. The man called back but received no answer. Apprehensively, the soldier left his post and headed into the guard house, apparently thinking the other guard had called him. This is what Ethan had hoped for. He sped up to the wall of the entryway. Moving low and treading lightly he crept beneath the window of the guard house. Just as he was nearing safety he slipped on the gravel, causing rocks to scatter.

"Did you hear that?" asked one of the guards.

"Yeah," said the other, "better check it out."

Ethan rushed out of the gate, and around the western side of the city walls. He had just enough time to make it far enough around the curvature of the wall to be hidden, when the guards came out of the gate. Breathing hard, Ethan pressed close to the wall. He'd planned on boarding one of the lifts and hiding there but, with the guards on alert now, he wouldn't be able to go unnoticed on the road. There was but one other choice and that was to climb down the side of the mountain. Committing to the less than desirable means of decent, Ethan set off. The going was slow. The side of the mountain was much steeper than he'd realized. He slipped several times, sending him careening down the side of the green giant. When he'd made it to the bottom, he was just inside the wood line, next to the road that ran to the Western Lookout. Up ahead he spotted the horse stable. No one was in sight so he made a run for it, crossing the wide-open road in the rising sun. Plastering himself to the stable wall, Ethan scooted along to the rear to look for guards but found none. Then he heard a voice inside the stable. The person seemed to be talking to the horses. The voice got louder and from the back corner of the stable Ethan saw a tall, dark-headed woman emerge, pulling a black horse along. She was taking the steed toward a solitary wagon upon which sat one box and one barrel. The lady bridled the horse and harnessed the mount to the front of the wagon. She patted the horse's side and headed back to the stable. Ethan took a chance. Betting that the wagon was being prepared for Deerborn's use, he darted toward it. The horse whinnied as Ethan neared. Running to the far side of the wagon Ethan rubbed the stallion's side as the woman had done. Once the horse was calm Ethan peered over the edge of the wagon. There was nowhere for him to hide in the back so he searched beneath, hoping for a better option. He found it. The belly of the wagon was fitted with wooden loops made for carrying items too long for the topside. Ethan crawled up through the foremost loop and slid his upper half into the back one. It was a bit uncomfortable but he was hidden well enough. He tucked his cloak up around himself to keep it from hanging too low and then he waited.

Soon, Ethan heard the gears of the massive elevator start to crank and turn and after a few minutes he saw the lift. Deerborn stepped off the platform, the woman met him half way, and together they walked to the wagon. Ethan's assumption had paid off.

"You are going alone then?" asked the stable keeper.

"Yes, I'm afraid so."

Deerborn sounded angry.

"Well then, the best of luck to you, Deerborn. Abril is in our thoughts."

"Thank you, Canton."

Deerborn climbed on the wagon and drove off without another word. Ethan readjusted himself for a tighter hold. Maintaining a good position proved much harder once the wagon began to move. Deerborn guided the horse along the road toward the Western Lookout. They were headed back towards Luminae. Ethan knew that Deerborn was going back to the Ancient's nest. The one where they'd heard the cave imps chanting '*NURRRR PLLLET*' from within the caverns below.

About midday Deerborn and Ethan arrived at the base of the western lookout. Ethan heard a familiar voice calling out to Deerborn. A man came up, whistling a sacred sounding tune.

"Good day, Deerborn. Pleasant day for saving one's wife."

"Indeed, Watts. Indeed. Are you ready?"

"Ready."

Deerborn wouldn't be entirely alone. The soldier named Watts, that Ethan met at the Eastern Lookout on his journey to Gloam, was going with Deerborn. This was probably the plan all along. Ethan remembered seeing Watts in town only the day before. Deerborn had most likely assigned Watts to the lookout post, expecting that Jukes wouldn't allow any soldiers to join him on the mission. He listened as Deerborn and Watts unloaded supplies from the wagon and then, together, they headed for the forest. Once they were far enough away, Ethan dropped down from wagon and slipped into the forest, trailing behind the other two.

...he spied a long rope dangling far over the edge...

Chapter Fifteen
Queen of the Colony

Ethan followed close behind Deerborn and Watts, staying just far enough away to keep from being discovered. The men traveled for the remainder of the day and made camp in the same spot that his party had the night after the attack of the cave imps. Ethan spotted a large tree with thick, low-lying branches. The enormous limbs would make a good resting place for the night. Ethan climbed the tree, found a suitable branch, and then took off his sword and pack. He used his carryall as a makeshift pillow and wrapped the cloak tightly to himself to ward off the late-autumn air. Finally he drew the sheathed sword in toward his chest, just in case he needed it at a moment's notice. He was very tired when rest finally came. Ethan gazed out toward the distant campfire wishing he could feel its heat. Situating himself differently to resist the temptation to be warm, Ethan turned to face the sky. The leaves of the tree were nearly gone now. Far above the tips of the furthest reaching branches, the Brother Moons sailed slowly and surely through the cloudless night. Over time they grew blurry and eventually Ethan fell into a deep and restful sleep.

The next morning Ethan awoke, head beneath his cloak, balled up against the trunk of the tree where it met with the branch. His sword and carryall had fallen to the ground, but luckily he hadn't. Sitting up he squinted through the bramble trying to get a look at the campsite. It was much harder to see in the light of the day and with the fire put out. Ethan dropped from the branch into a crouch and waited for any sign that his position had been compromised. When he heard no stirrings, Ethan picked up his belongings and moved silently toward the camp. Nearing the site, he realized that the men were already gone. Ethan knew that the soldiers were headed in a northwesterly direction and he started out after them.

By mid-morning the Glæmian spy found the cavernous hole that was sure to be the soldiers' target. Ethan had been led, more or less, by the growing call of the Nurplets. He was thankful that he hadn't run into them yet. Moving to the brink of the massive precipice Ethan sought out any sign of the men or their foe. Soon he spied a long rope dangling far over the edge about a quarter of the way around the newly formed canyon. Deerborn and Watts had already entered the Cave Imps' lair. Ethan rushed to the place where the rope was tied securely to a strong tree. Taking hold of the rope and gulping hard, he began his descent. Ethan had never been good with heights. The way down was slow and terrifying, but he kept his end goal in mind: helping Deerborn and saving Abril. The rope passed by only one entry point; Ethan pulled himself into the small cave and breathed a sigh of relief. In front of him the cavern sloped downward into the pitch black-- a scene all to familiar. Drawing his sword and pulling the hood of his cloak down over his forehead to conceal what would soon be his illuminated skin, Ethan disappeared into the cavern.

As he went, he discovered that the ground felt too moist, too sticky. The Glæmian bent low and pulled his glowing hand from his cloak, revealing the ground beneath him. The floor was covered in the purple secretion of the Cave Imps. Rising, he was more cautious than before, pulling his hood even lower. Continuing on, he had yet to see any forks in the cave; so, he was hopeful that he traveled in the right direction. The only noise, besides his sloshy foot-fall, was that of a constant dripping, reverberating throughout the tunnel. Soon, Ethan began to see a faint light up ahead and hoped that he'd caught up with Deerborn and Watts. He slowed his pace to keep a good distance from the light, just keeping it in sight. Ethan was close enough now that he could hear mumbled conversation between the two men. The ground shook subtly and the tunnel suddenly went dark ahead of him as the soldiers' torchlight was blown out by a rush of wind that shot up past Ethan. The gust brought with it a putrid odor. Ethan covered his nose and no sooner had he done so than the cries of Deerborn and Watts rent the silence. The ground shook again and the screams were gone.

Throwing his hood back to see more clearly, Ethan maneuvered quickly down the tunnel noticing, as he went, that his feet were heavier than before. The sputum was drying to the soles of his shoes. He slipped and fell, rear first, into the sludge, sliding a good twenty yards where he abruptly came to a slamming halt against a wall. It was a dead end. Standing,

Ethan readjusted himself. His cloak, once brown, now purple, had hardened but it saved his skin from the secretion. Ethan found his sword a few paces back up the tunnel; he bent to retrieve it. The hilt was sticky but he picked it up, all the same. Moving back to the dead end, Ethan felt around on the wall searching for a secret way through. He was sure that the wall must have moved aside, accounting for the rumbling in the passageway and the gust of wind. There was no noticeable way through. Feeling anxious and exposed, Ethan covered his shining face again. As he did, he gasped. A slender crack appeared in the wall and a cold blast of rancid air rushed out at him from within. Ethan inched toward the opening thinking that perhaps he'd accidentally stepped on the unlocking mechanism. Reluctantly, he placed his sword and glowing arm into the opening to see what lay beyond. Unknown to him, little pasty arms crept slowly out from the darkness at the same time, taking hold of his ankles. Ethan was yanked off his feet, landing on his back. The creatures began pulling at his legs and Ethan held fast to the opening. More came to join in the tug-of-war match. Finally the Nurplets bested Ethan and yanked him fully through the breach, down deeper into the tunnel.

Ethan writhed back and forth trying to free himself, but it did no good. Like in the wood, the shear number of the Nurplets was more than he could fend off. There were easily a hundred or more. They dragged him by his feet further and further into the belly of the earth. After a while he stopped screaming and fighting, realizing he was only wasting his energy. He knew he'd no doubt need his strength when the monsters stopped dragging him along.

The sounds of *NURRRR PLLLET, NURRRR PLLLET* fully enveloped the air.

Eventually the imps slowed and then stopped altogether. Ethan heard the voice of Deerborn yelling, "Undo us!"

"Deerborn!" shouted Ethan.

"Ethan?" cried Deerborn, "Is that you?" Then he was silenced.

A guttural voice rose from the darkness, speaking an unknown tongue. Ethan cowered at the sound.

"Who's...who's there?" mustered Ethan.

A croaky laugh rang through the underground hall.

Ethan couldn't believe what he was hearing. The creature sounded much larger than the tiny devils that forced him to his feet, trying to take the sword from his grip. But his hand was glued tightly to the hilt of his sword. The deep voice wheezed out what sounded like an order. He was pushed closer and closer toward the sound of deep wheezing coming from the darkness somewhere in front of him. Suddenly, large wet nostrils came within inches of Ethan's face. He was sure that he'd be gobbled whole at any moment.

More imps came now and, together, removed his cloak, tearing it from his body. Bright light poured into the room. The Queen was twice the height of Ethan. She squatted over what looked like a nest made of stones, blinking at Ethan with her pale, bulbous eyes. She laughed a deep, menacing laugh and soon the croaky laughter of the smaller imps filled the cavern. Her breath was horrible. Ethan gagged. An imp at his side bit his hand and he screamed. The Queen rose from her nest, revealing an underside like that of a pregnant sow. She'd been feeding infants, who dangled from her belly dropping at random and scattering deep into the cave behind her. Ethan could see that the enormous cavern was filling with even more imps, their calls and laughter growing more deafening by the second. Any moment, now, might be his last moment breathing.

Then a tiny flickering light passed across the ceiling moving quickly towards Ethan and the Queen. The room fell silent; all eyes watched the spectacle. The Queen was suddenly pierced in her fatty folds by a fiery arrow. She howled furiously as flames began to engulf her midsection. The room echoed and shook as the imps screeched in terror. Ethan turned and was shocked to see Delia near the rear of the hall, bow held high with another flaming arrow knocked. Mikael stood boldly next to her, sword and shield at the ready. The monsters behind Ethan began to scatter in fear. He was left alone with the burning queen. Ethan raised his sword and slashed bravely at the Queen's leg. His weapon met its mark. She tumbled over on her side howling loudly. His sword was lodged inside her thick upper leg. Ethan pulled maddeningly on his arm trying to free his hand from the adhesive that held his palm tightly to the hilt. With a sickening rip the sword finally came loose. Ethan cried out in pain. The flesh of his palm was badly torn, blood pulsing out. Ethan drew his arm close to his body and wrapped it in his tunic.

"Ethan!" shouted Deerborn.

The room was in a state of chaos, but Ethan found the Captain and Watts bound to the floor by the purple saliva of the imps purple secretion. Ethan ran to their side, dodging the ghostly looking creatures as they fell from ceiling above.

"My sword! I think you can get to it!" cried Deerborn, looking toward his weapon. "Hurry!"

Ethan followed his gaze and spotted Deerborn's sword on a nearby ledge. It was reachable. Retrieving the blade, he set to work releasing Deerborn as fast as he could. Ethan's hand was throbbing. When Deerborn's hands were freed, something grabbed Ethan by the ankle, from behind, and forced him to the ground. The Queen had latched onto him with her long purple tongue and was pulling him toward her open maw. The muscles in the monster's face were expanding and contracting in a relentless effort to swallow Ethan before the flames swallowed her.

"My sword, Ethan. Give it to me!" shouted Deerborn.

Ethan slid the weapon across the rocky surface to Deerborn. The bearded man flung it with great accuracy toward the writhing beast. The blade found its intended destination in the open mouth of the monster. The Queen released Ethan and began to tear at her neck as the sword was sucked further down her throat. Finally, the Queen gave up and dropped lifelessly to the ground, engulfed wholly in flames.

Delia and Mikael approached. Mikael freed Deerborn from the rest of his trappings and then went to work releasing Watts who was squirming relentlessly nearby. All around the humans, the Nurplets were dying. It was clear that they had been physically connected in some way to their queen. Watts was in far worse shape than Deerborn had been. His mouth was covered much like Abril's had been. Deerborn found his pack and pulled out several empty glass bottles. Then he sprinted off towards the dead and burning queen. Ethan knew exactly what he was doing. Mikael released Watts from the ground, who with a panicked look and muffled pleas, pulled helplessly at the facial plaster. One by one, Deerborn filled several bottles with the Queen's blood, contending with flames for a clear spot from which to retrieve the ichor. When the last bottle was corked, Deerborn reclaimed his sword from within the creature's charred throat and yelled, "I've got it! Come on, let's go!"

"But, Watts can't get this stuff off his mouth!" yelled Delia.

"Can you run, old friend?" asked Deerborn, rushing to inspect Watts.

He nodded.

"Very well," replied Deerborn. "We'll see about getting that abomination off your mouth at the surface."

Led by Ethan's brilliant glow, the party took off up the tunnel. Before leaving the Queen's hall, Deerborn snatched up the dead body of a Nurplet and threw it over his shoulder. Proof for unbelieving men.

* * *

At the surface, the battle weary company sat in a state of exhaustion. Deerborn and Mikael removed the purple snare from Watts' face. Ethan collapsed at the base of a tree, his mind settled on not moving for sometime. Delia sat down next to him and began tending to Ethan's torn palm.

"So," said Ethan, wincing as water made contact with his injury. "Thank you for what you did in there. I would have died. We all would have died."

"Welcome," said Delia focusing solely on the wound.

"I knew you were sneaky, but masterful with the bow and arrow, too?" laughed Ethan.

"Learned from the best," said Delia, eyeing Deerborn. "The training comes with the role."

"You are the daughter of the Overseer," said Ethan, flinching again.

"That, I am."

"But how did you know where we were?"

"Mikael and I followed you, of course."

"This is the second time in a week you've trailed me. You're really good at it."

Delia smiled.

"Good at getting in trouble," said Deerborn looking up from his work.

Delia's grin turned to a grimace.

"But all the same young lady, I thank you for what you did in there. You have the heart of a warrior."

"And the aim of one," added Mikael.

"And the aim," agreed Deerborn.

The men finished removing the last of the imp's poison from Watts' face.

"Thank you, sir," said Watts breathing in deeply. "And you, Mikael."

"Yes, Mikael, thank you for coming with Delia," said Deerborn. "If it were not for the two of you, we'd be lunch by now. Thank you for saving us."

"And hopefully we have saved Abril, as well," said Mikael.

Tears welled up in Deerborn's eyes as he clasped arms with the blacksmith.

"And you, Ethan Lambent," growled Deerborn, fighting away the tears. "Though I forbade you to come, that stubbornness that I remember all too well from Gloam, resurfaced in you... to our benefit." He smiled. "How did you follow us?"

Ethan explained how he'd ridden beneath the wagon and slept in the tree just outside their campsite.

"Remarkable. I had no idea," chuckled Deerborn. Then his expression became pensive. "Hmm, you are aware of the repercussions you will face for missing your entry exam, right?"

"I am," sighed Ethan. "It's worth it."

"I hope you're right," said Deerborn holding up a bottle of the Queen imp's blood.

After a well deserved rest and a hearty portion of their food rations, the company set out for Maridia, for Abril. Later that day, Watts began to show signs of fatigue much like Abril had before him.

Chapter Sixteen

A Song of Seasons

When the company returned to Maridia, one of the guards sprinted away from the gate, heading into the citadel. No doubt he had been instructed to alert Jukes of their return. Mikael ran ahead to get the Healer and, as the party entered town, Deerborn's guards saluted their captain with a disquieted expression. Jukes came stomping out of his home followed closely by the Rector. The Overseer's face went red when he saw his daughter. Ethan trailed behind Deerborn apprehensively. Jukes and the Rector both looked really upset. Delia tried to speak but was cut off by her father.

"Where have you been?"

"Mikael and I went to help Deerborn and Ethan," said Delia. "We saved..."

"Do not speak another word, child," interrupted Jukes, "We will discuss this later. Go indoors!"

"But father..."

"Now, Delia!"

With tears in her eyes Delia looked at Ethan one last time before running off toward her home. They would, most likely, not see one another again for a long time.

The Overseer eyed Watts. He was in worse condition, but Deerborn gave the soldier some of the Queen's blood on the way back and, in what was hopefully a response, Watts had not gone into a coma, yet.

"Watts, did you go with Deerborn, as well?" asked the Overseer in stunted disbelief.

Watts nodded unashamedly.

"Come, Deerborn, we must speak at once!" barked Jukes.

"I have the antidote for Abril," said Deerborn, so concerned with getting to his wife that he gave little notice to the Overseer's order. Jukes stepped in front of Deerborn, barring the way into the Captain's home.

"Did you hear me, Captain? You have defied direct orders by allowing another soldier to accompany you on your little outing and further you got my daughter mixed up in..."

"Now-is-not-the-time," interrupted Deerborn through gritted teeth.

"Unacceptable!" declared Rector Osric. "You dare speak to your Overseer with such defiance?"

Deerborn paid the Rector no mind as he stared hard at Jukes. The bearded giant looked ready to strike. There was noticeable fear in the Overseer's eyes.

"Further," continued Rector Osric, "you expect us to believe that you found the mythical creature you were looking for *and* retrieved its blood? Such nonsense!"

Never taking his eyes off Jukes, Deerborn pulled from his pack the lifeless cave imp that he'd picked up in their retreat. Without a word he threw it to the ground at the Rector's feet.

Jukes looked at the thing with an expression akin to horror. Flabbergasted, the man stepped aside.

"You cannot allow Deerborn to treat you like this," demanded Rector Osric, disregarding the creature.

"You found them!" exclaimed the Healer looking at the Nurplet as he and Mikael walked up. "Remarkable!"

Still silent, Deerborn entered his home followed by Mikael and the Healer who continued to remark about the creature as he passed by the stunned Overseer. Ethan almost slipped into the house unnoticed but he happened to meet eyes with Rector Osric just before he closed the door. The Rector's look was so frightening that Ethan feared more for his life in that moment than he had in all the darkest places of Gloam.

The company all went upstairs and circled around the bed in optimistic expectation. Deerborn carefully scooped Abril's head up in his arms and kissed her on the forehead. The Healer extracted a dropper of the Queen's blood and began to drip the antidote into Abril's open mouth. Ethan felt sick as he looked on. After a few, full droppers they laid the woman back down on the bed. In total disregard to those around him and with tears streaming, Deerborn began to sing to his wife. This is what he sang:

Sing a song of love, my lady,
Sing a song, my dear,
Of life anew in Springtime budding,
Sing of this, my dear,

Sing a song so tender, lover,
Sing a song, my dear,

Of kindling hearts in Summer hither,
Sing to me, my dear,

Sing a song, enduring partner,
Sing a song, my dear,
Of friendship lasting through the Autumn,
Sing with me, my dear,

Sing a life-long song, my lady,
Sing with joy, my dear,
Of welcomed rest when Winter endeth,
Sing our song, my dear.

"Do you hear me, my love?" cried Deerborn, "Do you hear *our* song? We are only in our Summer. There is still Autumn and Winter that we must weather together. Together! Do you hear? We haven't yet reached the end of Winter! Arise, my dear! Awake! I do not want to travel this life alone, my love! I do not!"

Though she still breathed, Abril did not wake that day, and all who were present wept bitterly with the broken man who had risked everything to see his wife smile on him once again.

Chapter Seventeen
Unprecedented Events

Though the darkness of Gloam had long since gone, the days that followed seemed nearly as loathsome as any Ethan had spent in Smarr's barren land. The evening of their return, after everyone had gone from the house, Ethan sat quietly in his room praying to the Creator for Abril's recovery. Deerborn remained by his wife's side across the hall. Because the house was so tiny, Ethan couldn't help but overhear the man as he spoke consoling words to Abril, then wept, then sat in silence, then the cycle would begin again. Ethan felt like he was intruding on sacred moments.

Later that afternoon, Deerborn startled Ethan, calling to him. Ethan crossed the hall and peeked through the crack in the door.

"Yes?"

"Come in, young man."

He somberly stepped into the bedroom.

"When Abril and I stayed with you, we often heard you and your family give thanks to the Light for His provision and your health."

Ethan nodded.

"Would you speak to Him now... for Abril?"

"I *have* been for hours, but I will gladly do it here with you now."

Ethan got down on his knees and Deerborn followed suit. Ethan began to pray for Abril as Deerborn wept, head buried in his hands. When Ethan finished, Deerborn, surprisingly, began to speak to the Creator himself. He spoke hopeful and desperate words. He spoke as if he, himself, believed...as the Glæmians believe.

Deerborn was interrupted by a knock at the front door. The broken man rose and tried to compose himself before descending the stairway. Ethan heard the front door creak open.

"What's the meaning of this?" said Deerborn.

"I'm sorry sir, but we are ordered to bring you to the Overseer," answered a timid voice.

Ethan hurried down the stairs to find four guards standing beyond the threshold. The men looked alarmed by the state of their captain, Deerborn's face still red.

"Very well," said Deerborn, adherently. "Ethan, look after her, will you?"

Ethan nodded, wide-eyed. "What's happening?"

"I have to answer for disobeying orders. I'll return soon. Thank you for what you've done," said Deerborn as he stepped into the street. "Everything's going to be fine. I'm sure of it."

* * *

Deerborn did not return. News spread quickly through the town that the Captain of the Maridian Guard had been detained until further notice. No clear reason had been given for his imprisonment, but no one thought Deerborn's violation of Jukes's order was equal to the harsh punishment he was receiving. Because Deerborn was respected and loved like he was, Maridians began dropping by the Overseer's home to demand an explanation. Aggravated by the constant callers, Jukes stopped answering the door. The only person allowed in the Overseer's home was Rector Osric. Soon, notices went up all over the citadel. The Overseer had scheduled a town meeting to answer the concerns of his people.

In the meantime, Ethan took care of Abril. His days were lonely but for the occasional visits of Mikael and, of course, the Healer who periodically stopped by to check on the unconscious woman. His only other companion was Poudis, poor company indeed, due to his constant state of moping since Deerborn had been taken. Ethan had seen no sign of Delia since they'd returned. There also had been no word from the Rector or from the university. He wondered if he'd missed his only chance to enter the school. Ethan tried to visit Deerborn but was unsuccessful in his attempt. The soldier named Blaise, who had helped Ethan train in sword fighting at the Eastern Lookout, told Ethan that Deerborn was not to receive any visitors as per the direct order of the Overseer. "Not even the guards are allowed to see the Captain."

"Why?" asked Ethan.

"None of us know why," replied Blaise. "But he is being held in our most secure cell-- a room with an iron door.

There's no way to see in or out. Deerborn is being kept far inside the guard house, in the holding cell that is rarely used."

"What? Why?"

"It's a mystery to me, as well! The only people who have seen the Captain since his imprisonment are the Overseer, Rector Osric and a guard who, oddly enough, hasn't reported for duty since that day. "

"Where did the guard go? Is he sick or something?"

"We don't rightly know... no one can find him! The whole thing is bizarre if you ask me, but we have to do as we're told or we'll end up in that dark cell, too!"

Try as he might, Ethan couldn't figure out why Deerborn was being treated so horribly. To be held in a cell was one thing but to be denied visitors *and* the light of day was, altogether, something else.

At weeks end the time had come for the town meeting.. In the hour proceeding the assembly, Ethan peered from a window to see people trickling into the middle of town, congregating near the fountain. When the hour was upon him, Ethan opened the front door to find the town-yard packed with people. There were people standing in the front doors, like himself, some, even, poking their heads out from upstairs windows. As he listened to the steady hum of huddled chatter, he realized that he'd never seen this many Maridians at one time. He wondered where they'd all come from. The meeting time came and went and still there was no sign of Jukes. The Maridians seemed to grow restless, pushing in towards the Overseer's front stoop. A few even knocked on the door: a sound Jukes was, no doubt, very accustomed to by now. Finally the door slowly opened and out crept Rector Osric. He looked worse than ever-- cheeks sunken, the circles beneath his eyes even darker than days before, lending to the most menacing of demeanors. The specter of a man raised his hands to silence the crowd, seeming unnerved when it did not happen immediately. Ethan noticed a letter of some sort in his hand.

"Where's the Overseer?" shouted someone in the crowd.

The Rector continued to hold his hands high, refusing to speak until the crowd calmed. The Maridians finally caught on and a hush fell over the town.

"The Overseer is sick and will not be addressing you tonight," boomed the Rector. "He has asked me to speak in his stead."

"Why is Deerborn being held?" shouted another citizen.

"The Captain of the Maridian Guard disobeyed a direct order from the Overseer and, as such, is paying the penalty for his actions."

"He was only trying to save his wife." said Watts as he stood at the back of the crowd. The soldier was looking much better than before.

"That's right!" rose another voice that Ethan knew all too well. "He's only tryin' to help poor ole' Abril!" said Miss Naava.

"Watts, is it?" interrogated the Rector, ignoring the librarian. "Let this be a lesson to you. Insubordination will not be tolerated among the ranks of the Maridian Guard. Would an officer kindly escort this soldier to the guard house?"

The guards looked at one another. They were unmoving and unwilling to obey an order from the Rector of Maridia's University.

"You don't have the authority to arrest me!" laughed Watts, mockingly.

"Ah, but I do," said the Rector, a satisfying smile breaking across his face. "By proclamation of the Overseer, I have been made second in command, as of this very day." He opened the letter he'd been carrying and held it high. "Come...see for yourself."

One of the officers on duty pushed through the crowd and approached Osric.

"It's true," said the soldier, inspecting the letter. "The Rector has been named Regent to the Overseer!"

As the voice of the crowd grew with concern, Watts' expression turned from one of triumph to defeat.

With great reluctance the order was given to apprehend Watts. The closest guard approached the recovering soldier and reached out for him. Watts pushed the man's hand away saying, "I know where the lockup is, Sorenson! No need to hold my hand!"

The crowd watched as Watts was escorted into the guardhouse. A few Maridians shouted at the injustice. But the people knew not what to do. Most were stunned to silence as nothing like this had ever happened before. An Overseer had never named a second to himself outside of his own family.

"Now then," began the Rector, victoriously. "Let us return to the matter at hand."

The citizens fell silent again, looks of concern in every eye.

"As I've already stated, Deerborn disobeyed orders and is now suffering the consequences. How long he will be held has yet to be determined. We wait on the Overseer's verdict. You will have more answers in the coming days."

The Rector unexpectedly turned and went back into the Overseer's house. Ethan, shocked by what had just occurred, stared blankly at the Overseer's front door. A curtain, cracked open, just above the door happened to catch his attention but no sooner had he noticed it than it was drawn shut.

* * *

The day after the town meeting, Ethan received a visit from a woman hailing from the university. She introduced herself as Professor J. Jury, the very person that was to administer the entry exam to Ethan before everything had gone awry. Ethan hadn't met any of the other instructors from the school and was surprised to find Professor Jury more than agreeable when compared to the man who had recently begun to find his way into Ethan's nightmares. And still, another surprise awaited Ethan.

"I am here to inform you that your entry examine has been rescheduled for the day after next," said the blonde-haired teacher, who stood only as high as Ethan's shoulders. "The appointment is dependent upon whether or not you are still interested in attending the school, of course."

"Of course," answered Ethan, "And yes, ma'am, I am still interested."

"Very good then. The Rector had thought that, perhaps, you would not be. And in the case that you hadn't, he wanted me to restate his um...excitement in having the opportunity to instruct you in your continued education."

"Really?"

"Those were his very words," stated the professor seeming to perceive Ethan's confusion.

"Well, if you say so. I thought that I had lost the chance to come to your school."

"Yes, and under normal circumstances you would be right in thinking so. This has never happened before: the Rector being so accommodating. Be thankful for another chance. And between you and me, it would be wise to stay in Rector Osric's good graces. If you do, it will make all the difference in your experience at the university."

"Thank you for the advice. I'll try my best."

"I'm sure you shall. I'm off then. See you in two days."

"Alright. See you then."

"Oh... I almost forgot. You'll find my classroom on the second floor at the very rear of the school, down the left corridor. And, please don't be late."

"I won't."

As Ethan closed the door behind Professor J. Jury, he couldn't believe that Rector Osric was being so "accommodating," as the woman described it. Perhaps the man wasn't angry after all. But, his gaze had seemed so hateful the day Ethan had returned with Deerborn. And he'd just imprisoned Watts for what seemed like no good reason at all. Further, Ethan wondered if the Rector was in some way responsible for Deerborn's treatment in the cell. Only time would tell if Ethan had been wrong about the Rector... only time.

Chapter Eighteen
School Days

The morning came for Ethan's entry exam. Heading over to the university earlier than expected, he navigated the lamp-lit corridors seeking out Professor J. Jury's classroom. Ethan passed the Rector's office and thankfully found the door closed. Anxiety and Rector Osric had become synonymous terms to Ethan and he was glad to not have to see the man before his test. He found Professor Jury's door opened. Entering the spacious room, he saw one long oak table in the center with benches of the same wood on either side. Above were two ornate chandeliers, identical to the one in the Rector's study. Candelabras lined the walls closest to the door and on the far side they stood between the tall, narrow windows which, from his standpoint, displayed a broken view of the Eastern Lookout far in the distance. The room was empty. Was he in the right place? At the back of the room was another open door. Inside was a stairway leading down to the first floor.

"Hello," called Ethan, down the echoing staircase. "Professor Jury?"

"I'll be there in a minute," replied J. Jury, from downstairs. "Go ahead and have a seat at the table, make yourself comfortable."

Ethan sat down and soon Professor Jury appeared in the doorway.

"Good morning, young man," said the cheerful woman. "Are you ready for the exam?"

"Yes, ma'am."

"Good, good. Though, I must apologize," said the Professor as she handed Ethan a thick stack of test papers. "The Rector...uh...I'm sorry-- the Regent, I really must get used to his new title. Anyhow, the *Regent* has put a lot on my plate for the day, so I will not be able to administer your exam. But, never fear, Regent Osric, himself, has agreed to monitor you today. He has never administered the entry exams for anyone. He must favor you. So it would seem that you're off to a good start!"

Ethan's heart sank, and he flinched as he heard the familiar booming voice at the stairwell door.

"Yes, Ethan, it would *seem* that you are off to a good start," said Rector Osric. "Let's see about keeping it that way, what do you say?"

"Y..yes, sir," stuttered Ethan.

"Very well then, shall we get started?"

Ethan wrote the date at the top of his exam and laughed. He'd not realized it, but today was his and Eisley's birthday. The events of the week had so filled his mind that he'd completely forgotten his birthday. A year ago this very day he and Eisley had begun their adventure. Ethan knew that Luminae was full to the brim with people celebrating the

Awakening. He wondered if Eisley was still there or if she was already on her way to Gloam.

"Happy Birthday, Eisley girl," he whispered as he began the test.

The examination lasted the entire day. Ethan was allowed periodic breaks after the completion of each subject. He excelled in the areas of arithmetic and grammar. In literature he did almost as well. He didn't know the Maridian poems and stories, yet he comprehended the selections in the test satisfactorily enough to answer the questions accurately. Even with all the recent cramming, Ethan only did fair in his history exam. There was so much about Maridian history that he didn't know. He expected such an outcome. It was in philosophy that he did the poorest, not being familiar with hardly any of Maridia's systems of logic. In fact, most of the logic seemed illogical to the Glæmian. This portion of the test was no doubt made harder by the constant glare of Rector Osric from the far end of the table. Ethan knew that the Rector was over the philosophy department, which meant he'd be spending a lot more time with the man.

Professor Jury returned near the end of the test. Once Ethan had completed it, he waited patiently for Rector Osric and J. Jury to determine his placement in the school. Ethan left the university with stacks of books and loads of homework. He had at least a month's worth of back work to do because it was so late in the term. Professor Jury also informed him that he'd be staying after class once a week to get extra tutoring in the two subjects that he scored lowest in. Ethan was happy to spend the extra time with J. Jury, but he was on edge at the thought of having to be alone with Osric ever again. Then there was the matter of Abril. Ethan would have to come up with a plan to care for her while he was at school. The Healer's wife had helped out once. Perhaps she'd be willing to do it again. Ethan didn't know many other people who might be free to watch Deerborn's wife except for, maybe, Delia, who he was sure wouldn't be allowed to come anywhere near him. And so Ethan resolved to ask the Healer's wife to find some other people for the task. Abril was loved in town, he knew that much, and he figured that finding others would be easy enough. As expected, the Healer's wife, whose name Ethan discovered to be Jes, found a handful of women that were willing to stay with Abril. Of course, Delia was not among them.

Ethan settled into a routine in the first few weeks of his studies. He was going to class four days. On Mondays, Ethan had arithmetic with the ancient looking Professor Fleming. Fleming was a hunched-back, plumpish sort of fellow with curly white hair and rosy cheeks. His students sometimes called him "Snow Beast," a name the Professor had become quite fond of.

On Tuesdays, there was history with J. Jury, and it was after her four-hour long class that Ethan would spend an additional two hours in private tutoring with her. He enjoyed Professor Jury's class, thinking she was knowledgeable beyond her years concerning the history of Maridia. Ethan began to learn more about the surrounding mountain-top towns, all of which he figured still stood, despite the other mountains having recently uprooted around them. One day in a tutoring session, J. Jury admitted that she was at a loss for why the mountains had disappeared.

"I've heard rumors, but nothing more. You know, the whole thing happened in the early morning hours so most of the town was still asleep. No one saw it happen, but we all felt it; and by the time anyone had gotten to the windows, the mountains were...well,they were just gone!"

Ethan remembered that the battle between the Ancients and Smarr had taken place just before sun up, because he and his family had watched the sun coming up over the horizon from on top of Smarr.

"To Maridians, the entire event remains an anomaly," mused J. Jury.

"But you're teachers, researchers, even," said Ethan. "Wouldn't you go study the giant holes?"

"Now, you would think so, wouldn't you?" said the professor.

Ethan nodded.

"Some of us tried. But it was a matter that the school faculty was expressly told not to waste our efforts on."

"But that doesn't make any sense," said Ethan.

"I agree. But the order came straight from the top, straight from Osric. Professor Niall and I confronted the Regent about his decision. We told him that it was entirely unacademic."

"What did he say?"

"He said that because he was the head of the natural philosophy department he would send a team to research the holes."

"Did he?"

"Not to my knowledge. If he had, I expect they would have run into the creatures you and Deerborn found. Perhaps, if he had, this whole mess with Arbil would have been avoided."

"Or it could have been worse," said Ethan. "The research team could have ended up like Abril."

"Too true."

As their private sessions continued, Ethan began to share with J. Jury everything he knew about the Ancients and she documented his stories. Of his journeys to Gloam, they spoke ,as well. Ethan shared his *Chronicle of Gloam's History and Culture* with her, instead of the Rector, as he'd originally intended to do. He'd decided weeks before not to show his findings to Osric because of the uneasy feeling he had around the man. Professor Jury's questions seemed unending, even when his answers had limits. In fact, the professor became so enthralled with the subject that she let Ethan finish his map for extra credit. He had nearly finished, one particular afternoon, when J. Jury interrupted him in the midst of drawing Smarr Mountain, as he'd decided to label Smarr on the map.[3]

---

[3] See End Notes, Reference #3

"All of your stories, are so...magical, so adventurous," said the woman. "I would like to show you something, if you would permit me to."

Ethan pulled his magnifying contraption off and rose to follow J. Jury out of the room.

Professor Jury led Ethan down to her office. Behind her desk, she pushed on a section of wall. The wall moved inward, revealing a hidden room behind it. Together, they entered into a small library.

"Wow," breathed Ethan, taking in the scene.

"These are all books of lore," whispered J. Jury, with a child-like gleam in her eyes.

"Really?" said Ethan, running his fingers across a few of the spines. Most of the books were so old that the titles had faded or the spines had fallen off altogether. He tingled with excitement.

"As you probably know, Osric doesn't want us to read these any longer. But, when I was a little girl, these were the only type of books I liked. It was no small joy to adventure with talking animals and færies. It is no small joy still."

She smiled. Ethan returned it.

"I know you are busy with school, but if you'd ever like to borrow any of these, I'd be happy to lend them. I could suggest a few, as well, when you're ready."

"Thanks," said Ethan. "Does anyone else know about this?"

"A few people. People I can trust," smiled the professor.

"Does Miss Naava know?"

"Of course, she knows. Helped me move and categorize them, actually!"

Though no law had been broken, J. Jury's collection would be very disliked by Osric. Ethan was certain that if the man knew about it, Professor Jury might possibly lose her job and it made him like her even more.

Wednesdays were literature days, taught by Professor Niall who was a beautiful, swarthy woman hailing from the northern-most reaches of the mountains. Only on a few occasions had Ethan seen people with such dark complexions; and only when they'd happened into Luminae, traveling from the north-most city in Glæm, called Eleora. Sadly, Professor Niall taught only from non-mythical sources, but for obvious reasons. Ethan liked the class all the same.

Thursdays, Ethan took philosophy with Rector Osric (determined never to call him Regent). He was astonished to find that the Rector paid him little mind in class and thus far the subject matter remained rather introductory. Ethan was thrilled to find out that it would be weeks before his and Rector Osric's private sessions would start. The Rector had been handed certain matters-of-state, being the recipient of an entirely new official position. On those sessions, Ethan was happy to wait indefinitely.

While the classes were running smoothly and everything was going better than Ethan could have hoped for at school, he felt more lonely than he'd ever felt in all his life. The students were all years older than himself and found no common ground with the Glæmian. Students were cordial with him, but nothing more. Normally this wouldn't have bothered Ethan. But in Glæm he'd always had the company of those he loved most. With his and Delia's friendship being forcefully severed, Deerborn in lockup, and Abril in her condition, there weren't many people for Ethan to confide in, if any. Besides J. Jury and Mikael, the latter of whom he'd seen only a few times when he'd been available to work in the smithy, Ethan was totally alone. Everyday he saw children, that he thought to be his own age, playing in the streets. But that was the problem-- they still acted like children, having not a care in the world. Ethan, coming from Glæm, was raised to become a man much earlier than Maridians were. He was sure they could be more mature if they wanted to, but perhaps their parents hadn't expected them to be that way at age fourteen. Either way, the cultural difference had created a gulf between him and what might have otherwise been his peers. Despite the loneliness, Ethan settled into a good routine and all seemed to be going fairly well; however, he couldn't help but think, with Osric running things as he was, that things might change.

Chapter Nineteen
A Chance Meeting?

Deerborn remained locked away without any word from either Jukes or Regent Osric concerning his release. In fact, Jukes hadn't so much as shown himself since he'd named Osric his second. Maridians began to wonder just how sick their Overseer was. Delia was rarely seen in town as well. Once, as Ethan was leaving Deerborn's, he had caught a glimpse of her entering her home-- a place that had become very mysterious in the last few weeks. Ethan heard the chatter concerning Delia, that on occasion someone would stop her in the streets to ask about her father. It was said that she'd spoken very little about his sickness but had looked exceedingly sad. Townsfolk began to regard her reaction as peculiar. Why had Delia been so quite on the matter? Why did no one seem to know what was wrong with the Overseer? The whole situation was a bit strange. Stranger still was that the Healer hadn't been called in to visit Jukes. He went to visit the Overseer one day, trying to get some answers to his neighbors' many questions. Regent Osric answered the door and told the Healer that Jukes was resting. When the Healer pressed the matter, wanting to examine his leader, Osric sent him away with a stern warning. This only weakened the already rocky relations between the physician and the Regent. Their distaste for one another had begun when the Healer requested the body of the cave imp that Deerborn had brought back. With it he thought he might begin to understand the species and perhaps find another way to help Abril. Osric had taken the body the day Deerborn tossed it to the ground. The Regent claimed that it had deteriorated days later and that he'd burned the remains, seeing no use in keeping what little was left of the creature.

When Ethan wasn't studying, he still spent his time watching over Abril, as he promised Deerborn he would do. In the early days of Abril's coma it was theorized that she would soon starve, not being able to ingest any sort of food. Yet, a fortnight after her long sleep began, she still appeared as healthy as ever. No one could explain why she was preserved like she was. One piece of information certainly seemed to be true from Dòmhnall's *The Whimsical World Unknown*: Abril was in a magical sleep of some sort. In Deerborn's stead, Ethan continued to feed drops of the queen imp's blood to Abril, as he was instructed to do by the Healer. He never really seemed to get over how sick it made him to do this.

Things seemed glum, indeed, in Maridia, with the exception of one fortunate turn of events-- Watts was released from his imprisonment and went back to his duties. He'd been stationed at the Eastern Lookout, near the Deadwood, ever since. It appeared that his detainment was only a show of Osric's newly acquired power.

One late afternoon, while leaving tutoring sessions with J. Jury, Ethan exited the university with his face buried in his history book-- a sight that was becoming commonplace to any that might wander past the university as classes let out. He was reading about the earliest known colonists to the mountain that would one day become Maridia. He was so focused on the account that he ran directly into someone.

"Ouch!" said a girl bending over to collect the belongings that dropped in the collision.

"Oh, I'm so sorry," said Ethan setting his open book on the ground to help collect the person's scattered items.

As Ethan bent down, he got his first look at the hooded figure. "Delia!" he said.

"Shhh," warned Delia. "Not so loud. If any of Osric's supporters saw you speaking to me, they'd tell Father."

"Osric's supporters?"

"He has eyes everywhere," said Delia, rising to her feet.

"How are you?" asked Ethan, standing with the girl.

"I've been better," whispered Delia, looking to her left and right for any sign of unwanted company.

"Is there anything I can do to help?"

"I'm sorry we can't speak right now."

Delia briskly walked away and Ethan began to pursue.

"Are you going to leave your book lying there?" asked Delia, turning to give Ethan one last look.

"Oh," said Ethan. He went back and swiped his book up off the ground, closing it quickly as he did. When he turned to address Delia again he saw the tail end of her cloak slipping through her front door and just like that she was gone.

Ethan walked back to Deerborn's, flustered at how badly the chance meeting with Delia had gone. Trying to put the event out of his mind, he set to work cooking up a stew. He was getting pretty good in the kitchen out of necessity. These days there was no one to cook for him. Once he added the meat, carrots, and potatoes to the stock and set the whole concoction to boiling in the pot above the fire, he lit a lamp in the sitting room and dropped into a chair. Trying to recall what he was doing before the encounter with Delia, he saw the history book on the table in front of him and remembered the story he was so caught up in. Grabbing the book, Ethan turned to the page he was reading. A small piece of paper fluttered out and to the ground. Curious, Ethan bent to retrieve the paper. Unfolding it, he read the following:

Tomorrow, before your class begins, go to our meeting place.

D.

D? D for Delia, of course! Ethan realized that she must have placed the note in the book when he laid it on the ground. No wonder she'd been so concerned with him picking up his book. But he'd closed it so fast that he hadn't noticed the note lying in it. He was thankful that it had actually stayed in the book. It might have been disastrous if the note was found by one of Osric's people. Whoever they were, they'd gone unnoticed by Ethan altogether. One thing was certain, though-- if Delia didn't want Osric's spies overhearing her, then she believed Osric was up to no good. And, if Delia believed Osric was up to no good, then Ethan should be more vigilant than he had been. Delia had asked him to keep his eyes open for suspicious activity but he was so busy with school work that he'd let his guard down. After all, Osric had paid Ethan so little attention the last few weeks. Whatever the case, Ethan would keep his eyes open now. And what of the note? Delia wanted him to go to their meeting place. They had met only once at the tombs. But surely if Jukes and Osric had people watching Delia, she wouldn't be able to get to him. The meeting would be found out and stopped. The odds seemed to be against them. But Delia was really sneaky. Somehow she managed to beat him to the graves. Maybe she knew a secret way out of the city. She would be there, despite the odds. Ethan knew it and he would be there, too.

The next morning Ethan woke with excitement. He dressed quickly, ran his fingers through his disheveled hair, and bolted down the stairs. At last, he'd know what was really going on in the Overseer's house. At last, everything would be revealed. The gates were just being opened for the day when Ethan arrived at them.

"G'morning, Ethan," said a soldier.

"Oh...good morning, Blaise," answered Ethan, recognizing the man.

"Where are you off to so early this morning?"

"Er...I just wanted to...to visit my ancestor's grave."

"Very well, then. Good day to you."

"You, too. Oh...how's Deerborn doing?" whispered Ethan.

"We're not allowed to see him yet, but he's still kicking," answered Blaise in a mirrored hush. "In fact," he said, lowering his voice even more, "he sounds better than ever."

"Really?" asked Ethan.

"Really. Been humming tunes all day long, he has. Go figure."

"Yeah...go figure."

"Don't be late for school today, young man," raising his voice loud enough for the soldiers in the guard house to hear.

"Um...no, sir, I won't."

Blaise winked, Ethan smiled and ran on his way. He traveled out through the thick morning fog to Earnest's grave. He thought when he rounded the corner that Delia would be standing there. She wasn't. Ethan crouched against the side of the tombs and resolved to wait as long as he must. The sun moved across the eastern sky, steadily striding towards its welcomed friend: the western horizon. Still, Delia didn't come. About midday Ethan knew she would not appear. Had that actually been her note or something that had been left in the book by previous owners? Yes, it was definitely her note. Who else could have written it? Something must have kept her from getting to him.

Downcast and hungry, Ethan re-entered the citadel. He stopped to ask Blaise if there had been much traffic through the gate that morning. Blaise looked curiously at Ethan and said that there had been no one but himself through the gate the whole morning. Ethan went back to the house to retrieve his books for the class he was late for and, with pang of realization, he remembered that it was Thursday! He'd missed half of the philosophy class! The Rector's class! He debated not going at all, even pretending to be sick, but he thought this might be worse for him. He'd not missed a day of school yet and he'd kept up with all of his assignments. But if ever there was an excuse for Osric to keep Ethan after school, he would have it today, unless, Ethan could get there in time to finish the class. He was so unnoticed in philosophy class that he thought there might even be a chance that he could slip in without the professor knowing. It was midday; they would be breaking from class to eat. He could just slip back in with the other students and take his seat like normal. It was a shot in the dark but it was all he had. Stuffing the right books in his carryall and then stuffing his mouth with a big piece of slightly stale bread, Ethan darted off toward the university.

...his eyes seemed to burn...

Chapter Twenty
Turn for the Worse

Ethan got to the school just as the students were filing back into their classes. Merging with the crowd, Ethan slipped into class and into his desk in the middle of the room. A young woman sitting to his left, whose name he thought to be Jocelyn, gave him an inquisitive look but said nothing. Then the Rector came in, already teaching as he shut the door behind him. He stopped in mid-sentence and looked inquisitively toward Ethan, who tried to play it off by writing down what Osric had just said. He acted surprised to see Ethan, but nothing more. The Rector resumed his instruction and, in his typical manner, took long-legged strides toward the front of the room. Class continued like every class before it and, as usual, the Glæmian wasn't even given a second notice.

Jocelyn slid Ethan her notes from the part of class he missed. It was the first real interaction Ethan had with any student thus far. The gesture had both surprised and warmed him simultaneously. He nodded thankfully at the young lady and began jotting down the missed instruction. Hastily, he returned them to the their owner while managing to keep notes of the lesson at hand. Just when Ethan thought he was in the clear, the Rector did something he'd never done before.

"Ethan," rumbled Osric. "earlier, I said that all things in nature are equally dependent upon the total structure. What else did I say about that structure?"

Osric's beard seemed to fan out as the grin beneath it was born. The withering man would try to make a display of Ethan after all. But thanks to Jocelyn, Ethan was prepared.

"Um...I believe you said that, 'nature is only the way the character of the total structure manifests itself at a certain point in time and space,' right?" answered Ethan reading from his notes.

Osric's smile was short lived, for no sooner had it seen the light of day than it also met its death. Osric moved in a slow and calculated manner towards Ethan's desk, and picked up his notes. Ethan couldn't see the Rector's face because his notes were blocking his view, but when Osric dropped the page, his eyes seemed to burn. Those fiery eyes darted back and forth around the classroom. He began to examine the notes of the students around Ethan. Again, Ethan was prepared for this. He hadn't copied the notes word for word. He even left out things that he thought he could remember. So there was no way Rector Osric could link his notes to Jocelyn. But Jocelyn didn't know this and, when Osric made it to her desk, she looked like she was going to be sick. Osric took note of her sickly appearance and that evil grin resurfaced. He thought he had found the culprit. But, after comparing her notes with Ethan's, the smile vanished again. He put down both copies of his lecture, turned quickly and strode back to the front of the classroom.

"You-are-correct-Ethan," forced the Rector. "Can you explain to me what that means?"

Ethan didn't know. The statement he'd read aloud from his notes had confused him. He was speechless.

The Rector leered at him.

"It means," answered the Rector, "that everything in nature is connected and dependent upon all the other parts. It has always been this way. I'll say it again: *Everything* is *dependent* on *everything* else."

Ethan didn't like where this lecture was going. He felt a tinge of warning in the back of mind.

"What this means, is that nothing exists that is independent from the whole. This is what naturalists know to be true."

Ethan swallowed hard.

"There are some that believe otherwise," said Osric. "Isn't that right, Mr. Lambent?"

Several people eyed Ethan, as if waiting for a reply from him. He said nothing and couldn't bring his eyes up from his desk. Finally, it was happening. Osric gave an amused sort of chuckle under his breath. Ethan might have outsmarted the Rector before, but the man wasn't going to let a Glæmian have the last word.

"Yes," began Osric again. "There are those in this world who believe that *something*... or should I say, *one thing* is independent from all the rest."

There was a long pause. Ethan chanced a glance at his professor. Victory is what Osric's expression said. Victory!

"We will discuss the nonsensical view next week. Class dismissed."

Ethan collected his things and rose from his seat, trying as best he could to exit the class without any further attention on himself.

"And where are you going?" said Osric, just before Ethan made it into the hallway.

Ethan turned around slowly. "Sir?"

"How was your morning? Did things go as you expected them to?" That grin was back.

Ethan gaped.

"Hmm...I would say that is a no. Well, be that as it may, I say it's high time that you and I begin our tutoring session. Don't you?"

"Yes...sir," answered Ethan.

"Good then. I am free now. What say we get started?"

Ethan's heart sank. The thing he dreaded most was coming to pass. Defeated, Ethan walked back into the class and shut the door behind him.

Chapter Twenty One
The Incubus of Anxiety

The tutoring session with Osric wasn't exactly what one might think of when one imagines tutoring. Ethan was left alone for two hours to rewrite, as many times as possible, the notes he had taken in class. The ones that Osric knew Ethan had copied from someone else. All in all, the chore was a waste of time more than it was a severe punishment. Osric left shortly after he'd given the assignment, appearing too disgusted to remain in the same room with a person of such "nonsensical" views of the world. Ethan knew the next philosophy class was going to be the hardest thing he'd actually faced since being alone in the darkness of Gloam. The encounter with the imps and their queen wouldn't come close. What plagued Ethan's mind the most was that Osric found out about the planned meeting with Delia and then kept it from happening somehow. The Rector had an unknown stake in keeping them apart. But why? Perhaps he did not want Ethan to know what Delia knew. What was Rector Osric doing? Was Delia okay? What part did Jukes have to play in the matter? The questions flooded his mind as he sat and laboriously copied his notes for two grueling hours. When the "tutoring" was over and Osric returned to inspect the work, Ethan was finally released. Without a single word to the

Rector, he left the school, going directly home, to his room, to his bed, and into a flood of nightmares.

He dreamt of a room as dark as night. He felt the warmth of Eisley's hand in his own, next to him. Ethan knew, or rather felt, that there was something in the room besides he and his sister. He could feel it breathing. Light flooded the room and he saw two large Squalor, like the one he killed in Gloam. They stood poised to strike! Saliva-covered fangs spread wide! He tried to run but they pounced on his back pinning him to the ground. He saw the doorway to the outside world from where he lay. Eisley stood there, backing away from him. Behind her he saw an ancient, glowing brightly, but the dream distorted the ancient. It looked far too small. The creature whisked Eisley up and he was left alone with the Squalor. The heavy paws with their razor-sharp claws dug, deep, into his back. He felt his own blood running down his sides. Trying to get a final look at his bane, Ethan turned to see, not the Squalor, but rather...Smarr. Ethan screamed. Smarr laughed a deep rumbly laugh. The heavy weight of his mountainous talons pushed Ethan further and further into the ground. Beneath Ethan, the ground erupted with cave imps, spewing forth like ants. He was smothering but couldn't tell whether it was from the weight of Smarr's giant paw or from the sea of imps crawling out from below him. The ground finally gave way and Ethan tumbled into a cavernous hole, slamming breathlessly into the bottom. There he lay in complete darkness, his own light shining dimly. Out of the deep came Rector Osric walking slowly towards him. The man looked like a corpse; his lips moved like the mouth of a puppet. An eerie whimpering sound came from the dead-man's lips. Then, Ethan heard a deeper voice still. A voice as old as the earth said, "Look to the brothers for your answer!" Ethan's scream echoed through the cave. He screamed until he heard himself screaming, which woke him. Poudis stood over him whimpering much like Osric had in the dream. Ethan found himself on the floor with the concerned D'mune licking his forehead. The room was full of floating feathers. Confused, he rose to find that his pillow had been ripped to shreds. He could still hear the old voice in his head.

"Look to the brothers for your answer?" he said aloud to himself.

The day that followed the nightmares, was much like a dream itself. He went to work in the smithy but couldn't focus on his task. He was so tired from the restless night-- the dream kept replaying in his mind: the room, his sister, the squalor, the strange-looking ancient, Smarr, so many Nurplets, Rector Osric, and, of course, the riddle-like statement. He knew it was only a dream but he couldn't help but wonder if Eisley was okay. He also knew he'd never look at Osric the same way again. As if the man wasn't creepy enough, Ethan now had this new image of the Rector to contend with.

Mikael inquired about Ethan's mood.

"Bad dreams last night is all," answered Ethan, who'd been hammering at the same spot on the blade for some time. The section of blade was flattened like a pancake. "Sorry about that," said Ethan, raising the fledgling sword.

"Not a problem," said Mikael. "Why don't you go home and get some rest."

Ethan complied and put away his tools. As he was leaving he turned and asked, "Mikael, are there any...brothers in Maridia?"

"Brothers? What do you mean? Like, are there any Maridians who are brothers?"

Ethan nodded, a little embarrassed by the question.

"Why do you ask?"

Ethan explained what he heard in his dream.

"Well, I suppose there are many. Let me think. Um... Ah, yes! Oleg, the tailor, has a brother named Vonkel. A few of the soldiers are brothers..." the list went on and on.

"You know...never mind," said Ethan, rubbing his temples. "I'm sure it was only a dream."

"You're probably right, Ethan. Go get some rest."

"Thanks."

There were, obviously, too many brothers in the city to go to one by one and ask for...for what? For help? What sort of help? Ethan laughed at himself. It was only a dream. Surely if the old voice had meant to be of any help its message would have been clearer.

Ethan returned home, checked on Abril, and then crawled back into bed for some much-needed rest. That rest that did not come.

* * *

As the following week unraveled, so did Ethan. Every time he nodded off, he had the same dream. Every time, he awoke screaming. He didn't know why he kept seeing the same scenes played over and over again in his mind. What he did know was that a great anxiety over the coming class with Rector Osric began to build within him. Ethan had no one to really confide in. He'd shared parts of the dream with Mikael; yet, he didn't feel like he knew Mikael well enough to share everything. Perhaps as time went by he might, but not yet. Professor J. Jury noticed that something was wrong with Ethan in class on Tuesday and asked him about it afterwards. Even with the professor, Ethan didn't feel like he could be fully honest. After all, her boss was a major part of the problem. Besides, she'd probably think him crazy. So he kept the feelings to himself. He was alone and, to make it worse, the old voice had crept out of his dreams and into waking reality. He began to hear, "Look to the brothers for your answer," while cooking, while studying, and even while walking around town. He started thinking that he *was* going crazy. What was happening to him? His whole world seemed to be crumbling at the edges. And there was still Rector Osric's class to contend with on Thursday.

Chapter Twenty Two
A Showdown of Minds

Ethan woke with an overwhelming sense of uneasiness. The time had come for his beliefs to be challenged in the classroom. From the day he'd sat in the Rector's dark study, he knew this moment would come and he was ashamed to admit he feared it. He did not fear losing his faith, no-- he was far beyond that. One does not radiate the light of their Creator and simply cease to do so. What Ethan feared was the rejection of his classmates and, as strange is it may seem, the rejection of the Rector. Despite his nightmarish qualities, he was the head of academia in Maridia, and if Osric belittled Ethan then the school might, as well. All of his professors would most likely shun him: Snow Beast, Niall, and, worst of all, J. Jury. He thought back on how uneasy his grandmother felt about his move to Maridia. Perhaps the coming encounter had been why she'd felt that way. What if Jaine had had a premonition of sorts?

Ethan entered his class, along with all the other students. The Rector was already sitting at his desk in the front of the room. Again, the man looked but a shell of what he'd once been. Osric's eyes were glossed over with a milky film. But he glared at Ethan through those cloudy eyes. As soon as everyone had taken a seat, the professor began.

"We will now continue our study from last week."

Osric stood.

"Naturalism. Naturalists believe that nothing exists outside what can be perceived by our senses."

He began to pace at the front of the room.

"This is the time honored position that I and all the Rectors before me have proudly held to, here in our university."

Moisture began to form on Osric's forehead. He tugged at his collar.

"There is another view. A view I began to expound on in our last class."

He looked directly at Ethan, again.

"*Super*naturalism. The supernaturalist believes that things can exist beyond what we can perceive with our senses."

Someone at the rear of the class snickered under their breath. An austere looking man in the front raised his hand.

"Yes, Taibon?" said the Rector.

"Are you referring to those who believe in the existence of a creator?"

"Precisely, Taibon."

Jocelyn raised her hand.

"Yes?" said the Rector, pointing at her.

"My family has never referred to its beliefs as naturalism, but we are naturalists by your definition."

"As are all Maridians, Jocelyn," answered the Rector. He began to lecture again but Jocelyn's hand shot back up. Osric seemed to be growing impatient. "Yes," he said with a hint of annoyance.

"But, I know of Maridian families, including my own, that say *nature* created everything," said Jocelyn.

"Some do *think* that. I would not deny that it is a possibility," answered the Rector.

"Would that not be an existing creator, then?" said the young woman.

"Yes...but one *within* the confines of nature not from *without*. That creator would be a part of the total structure that I spoke of last week."

"I see," answered Jocelyn.

"Your inquiries, Jocelyn, are confirming my position," said Osric. "Do you know that there are actually people in this world, today, that hold the supernaturalist view point? In fact, there is one among us, even now, that does."

The Rector stared hard at Ethan.

Most of the class followed Osric's gaze.

"Why don't we ask Ethan Lambent his view on the matter?"

This was the moment of truth. Surprisingly, Ethan's fear had been replaced with boldness. In fact, as is usually the case when one finally meets with an expected obstacle, one begins to wonder why they spent so much time worrying in the first place. Anxiety has only ever served to waste mankind's time.

"I believe in a Creator," said the Glæmian, calmly.

"Is the creator you believe in outside the confines of nature or not?" said Osric.

"He's outside of nature, of course. He made it all."

Osric's reaction was as close to elation as such a decrepit man might muster.

"Ah, you see class," smirked Osric. "This is what the Glæmians believe."

He began to pace back and forth again, locking his hands together near his chest.

"I've been there, I've walked the streets of the so-called *Shining City,* and studied from their tomes. The people there have this odd notion that they are different from you and me. That they are more special because they claim to *know* a creator."

"We don't think that..." began Ethan.

"You would deny that your people think they are better than those outside of Glæm?" interrupted the Rector.

"Well, some might," said Ethan. This was most certainly true. Ethan had struggled with his townsfolk not accepting Canis because he was an outsider.

"There! You see class! He admits it!"

"We're humans. We still make mistakes," said Ethan.

"That's right you *are* human. *Only* human," said Osric.

"Yeah, only human... with the *Creator* living inside me!"

"The idea of an all powerful being standing outside of nature is simply illogical! Intolerable even!"

"Don't you see that your viewpoint would fall apart if there were but one proof of such a Creator?" laughed Ethan.

"If there were but one...there is no such proof," said Osric taken aback by Ethan's challenge.

"What of the world around you, professor?" said Ethan rising from his seat. "In all of its grandness! Is that not evidence enough?"

"Perhaps evidence of nature as creator, which would be a part of the total structure!"

"Nature? Really? I heard the Overseer speak of this idea once. But it falls apart so easily."

"How so?"

"Would you agree that everything in nature has a beginning?" asked Ethan. He didn't know where these ideas were coming from but they continued to form solidly in his mind.

"I would."

"Then how could nature have created itself?"

"There are many theories concerning how things might have come to be. Most of them valid."

"Like...a Creator?"

"Of course not!"

"Then what?"

Osric was pulling at his collar again and rolling his head at alarming angles but still he continued.

"I do not have to placate you, Ethan. That topic is outside the scope of this lecture."

Then others began to raise their hands. They wanted to hear the theories, as well.

"Very well," conceded Osric, as he pulled down on his robe as if situating it. He seemed very uncomfortable. "But before I go on, *you must sit down, young man.*"

Ethan, not even realizing he was on his feet, sat back down.

"Now then. One *credible* theory is that billions of years ago there was a spontaneous eruption caused by the right mix of particles..."

"Where did the particles come from?" interrupted Ethan. "Nature? Did nature create the particles before nature created itself?"

"That's it! No more! Whatever the case, little boy, I will *never* concede to the foolishness of an all-powerful being having made anything! It is preposterous!"

The class seemed to be expectantly waiting for Ethan to reply.

"What if I could prove you wrong?" he said. But he'd let this slip from his mouth prematurely.

"How?" growled Osric.

Ethan knew he'd have to give an answer now, though it might sound foolish. It had once sounded foolish even to him. "The Creator places His light within any who trust in Him," he said, more meekly now.

"You mean to say you glow in the dark?" Osric's triumph rose as it was fed by the fires of the class laughter.

"That's exactly what I mean," said Ethan.

"Show us then, boy! Ah...but you cannot? Even if it were true, there is no darkness here," laughed Osric. "How convenient for you."

Ethan, silently, lowered his head. There *was* no way for him to prove himself in that moment. He needed total darkness to shine out. He should not have pushed the matter as far as he had. Now he'd made himself out to be the fool.

"I should have known better than to allow such ignorance into this university. Remove yourself from this institute and do not return," said Osric, with too much calm. It sounded almost rehearsed.

Ethan picked up his carryall and chanced a look at Jocelyn, who sat as he had, looking at her desktop. He turned to see that many of the students mirrored her pose. Without a word, Ethan left the class, closing the heavy door behind him. Everything he feared might happen had just unfolded before his very eyes.

Chapter Twenty Three
He Waits for No Man

Ethan went back to Deerborn's home. There he remained in the company of only Poudis for...hours? Days? Ethan wasn't sure. The only sounds he heard were those of a settling house, a snoring D'mune, and the voice inside his head continuing to say, "Look to the brothers for your answer." Finally he was roused by a knock at the door. Professor J. Jury stood in a light rain. It was very rare that rain fell at all, but, given the occasion, it represented Ethan's mood, perfectly.

"May I come in?" asked J. Jury.

"Oh, sure. Sorry," said Ethan. "I guess I'm not all here right now."

"Understandably," said the professor as she removed her raincoat, shaking it off at the door. "So, tell me. What happened?"

Reluctantly, Ethan began to recount the day's events. When he finished, J. Jury stood with a determined look.

"Just unacceptable!" she proclaimed, patting Ethan on the shoulder. "I will see what I can do to persuade the Regent to let you return."

Ethan nodded and the professor left. He knew he'd never return to the university if Osric had anything to do with it. He wasn't sure he even wanted to go back. How could he look any of the students in the eyes again? If only there were a way to prove he had a light within him.

Despite the encounter with the Rector, restful sleep finally came to Ethan. For the first time in a week he didn't dream at all. Ethan woke suddenly the following morning because of yet another knock at the door. He suspected that it was Professor Jury returning to give him the bad news. He was surprised, even shocked, when he opened the door, to find Alaric and Delia Jukes.

This time, Ethan was a bit more aware of his manners. "Come in," he said still startled by his visitors. Jukes looked like Jukes. No rings under his eyes, no sunken cheeks, no pallid skin, no sickness to speak off. Ethan had begun to imagine that Jukes bore the same sickly appearance as the Rector. He did not.

"How are you, dear boy?" asked the Overseer. Delia stood silently by his side and curtsied after her father had greeted Ethan.

"I'm...okay, I guess," managed Ethan.

"That's not what I hear," said Jukes. Ethan detected a slight strain in Jukes' voice.

"How are you?" asked Ethan of Jukes.

"Much better now. Much better."

"Really? But, you've been sick for so long."

"Strangest thing happened yesterday. In the late afternoon the whole sickness just seemed to...disappear. One moment I was confined to my bed, barely able to squeak out a word, the next moment it felt as if a heaviness had simply been snatched right off of me. I don't know how to explain it. But enough about me. Don't you worry about anything. We will get you back into the university."

"University?" said Ethan. "I don't care about the university. What about Deerborn? He's still in prison. Osric said he was still being held there by your will! Why?"

"I can't explain that either, Ethan," said Jukes, a disturbed look settling on his face. "I know that I gave the command to keep Deerborn incarcerated. I know it because I remember saying it. But I didn't come from me. I know that really doesn't make any sense. But what I wanted to do and what I did were two different things. Last night was the first time I was able to speak my own thoughts since I became sick."

Jukes sat, downcast. Delia placed a hand on her father's back. "It really is amazing how much different father is today! He's a different person, altogether."

"Well, what do you think caused it?" asked Ethan.

Both Jukes and Delia shrugged.

"What about Osric? Did you really want to make him Regent?" asked Ethan.

"Unfortunately, I did that of my own accord," lamented Jukes. "I was so confused about the cave imp that Deerborn brought back. I began to question everything I thought to be true, but Deerborn still had to answer for not obeying orders. Having often sought advice from Osric, I went to him with my concerns. He became so angry at the thought of me even toying with such questions as the validity of the books of lore..." he looked up at Ethan, "and the validity of your beliefs."

Ethan felt a great relief wash over him in that moment. Finally, someone, the Overseer of all people, was actually taking his beliefs seriously.

"As I said, Osric was so angry. In a moment of cowardice I gave into Osric's demands," said Jukes. "He suggested, as a show of force, that I imprison Deerborn for a few days and I agreed to it. I should have never listened to him. I know that now. As you well know, most of the town turned on me for that decision. I should have owned up at that point but, instead of facing my horrible choices, I followed Osric's council, yet again, and made him my second in command. It seems that if you give Osric even one inch, he will take a mile."

The Overseer stood from his hunched position and a healthy pride seemed to fill him. "Everything will be made right. Deerborn shall be released, but first I must deal with Osric. I will strip him of his new title of Regent and of his position as Rector. Professor Jury came to me late last night. She had gone to talk with Osric about reinstating you in school. When she arrived at his office, she overheard him inside talking to someone. Jury said that he was babbling on about needing more time, more chances. She said he kept repeating that he wasn't useless...that he could get the job done. When she knocked on the door, she said the conversation ended and after a few moments he opened the door. The room was empty except for himself. He'd been talking to himself!"

"What?" said Ethan.

"I couldn't believe it either," said Jukes. "He's lost his mind and I intend to make sure he causes no more harm. In fact, one of the guards is probably detaining Osric this very moment. I've ordered Blaise to bring Osric to my home. I am going this very minute to deal with him."

Jukes turned to leave and Delia started to follow. Jukes stopped and seemed to consider his daughter for a moment. "Dear, why don't you stay with Ethan while I take care of this situation."

Delia smiled and hugged her father.

Jukes gazed momentarily at Delia and Ethan, standing next to one another. With a smile and a slight nod he turned and headed out with gusto.

Delia went to the window to see her father bounce off across the center of town toward his destination. She ran to Ethan and threw her arms around him. It was wonderful beyond description just to be in the warm embrace of another. It had been so long since he'd felt the all encompassing warmth that accompanied his mother's, his father's, his sister's embrace.

Ethan and Delia talked about everything that had happened in the weeks they spent separated. Delia had, in fact, been detained by her father, under the orders of Osric, no doubt, on the morning she was supposed to meet Ethan at the tombs. At that meeting she planned to tell him of the strange persuasion Osric held over her father. She wanted to tell him of Jukes' helplessness. She knew her father well and knew he would not, willingly, continue holding Deerborn in prison. They spoke of these things and many others when they were silenced by a shattering sound and an ear-splitting scream that pierced the late morning air.

Chapter Twenty Four
Out of the Fray

Ethan and Delia ran straight for the door and into the streets, hand in hand. A crowd was forming in front of Delia's home. Moans and cries rose from the crowd that encircled something. Ethan saw it first, though before it had registered Delia screamed, "No...no!" An upstairs window in the Overseer's home was shattered. Delia released Ethan's hand and sprinted into the throng of onlookers. Ethan tried to catch her but she was already gone. Pushing his way through the people, he found Delia bent over the broken body of Alaric Jukes.

"Guards, arrest this man! He has killed our Overseer!" shouted Osric, bursting out of the Overseer's front door.

Osric was on the stoop now, single-handedly detaining Blaise: the very person Jukes had sent to detain the Rector. Blaise was kicking and struggling to free himself but Osric held fast. All was chaos. The guards struggled to apprehend Blaise, thrashing about as he was.

"Gag him!" shouted someone in the crowd, and oddly, one of the soldiers did so.

In the brief moment between Osric removing his hand from Blaise's mouth and the soldier filling it with cloth, Blaise managed to get out one word: "Lies!" he shouted and then he was silenced again.

Delia got to her feet, eyes aimed at Osric. She began to move towards him, slowly at first, and then she broke in to an all-out dash. Ethan tried to stop her but she pushed him away.

"You did this to my father!" she shouted. "*You* did this." She was hitting Osric with all she had in her. Ethan tried again to pull her off the man but Osric was attempting to restrain her, as well. Osric won out by pushing Ethan off the stoop sending him into the mud. Holding tight to Delia, Osric shouted, "Guards, get this girl inside her house. She's suffered a great loss today and is clearly delusional."

More guards came and took Delia into the house. She was a blur of kicking and screaming and hair. Ethan jumped up and ran at Osric himself, anger building inside him. He knew Blaise hadn't killed Jukes. Osric had. Before he reached the murderer, a powerful arm seized him from behind and dragged him away from the fray. Ethan squirmed and kicked and managed to smack the man in the nose with the back of his head. The man hollered angrily and then everything went black.

Chapter Twenty Five
Revelations

Images flashed-- memories filling Ethan's mind. At first, many of them. Then, fewer and fewer and finally his mind fixed itself upon one memory in particular. He was standing in his front yard with his father, looking towards the night sky. Miland, Ancelin and Vergance sailed towards the horizon. He heard his father speaking, muffled at first, but as Ethan honed in on the memory, Amory's voice rung out crystal clear.

"You know, the Celestions are saying that the moons and the sun will all align with us. Grandpa says that hasn't happened in over a millennium. It's expected to happen sometime in the coming months."

Then Ethan heard another voice, the old voice, now so familiar. "Look to the brothers for your answer!"

Ethan jolted up with a start.

"The Brother Moons!" he shouted. He remembered now. The moons were supposed to align, causing the day to be as night. Real night. This event is exactly what he needed to show Osric, once and for all, that the light inside of him, the Light of Glæm, was real. The Rector would have his proof. Ethan's head throbbed. But why? Then with horror he remembered what had happened. Jukes was dead and Blaise was to blame. Delia was being held in her home. What about him? He was lying in his room. Ethan darted out of his door and down the stairs. He flung open the front door to find his way blocked. Two unfamiliar Maridian Guards stood there.

"Back inside," ordered one.

"Why won't you let me pass?" asked Ethan.

"Orders of the Overseer," returned the man.

"But...the Overseer's dead."

"Orders of the *new* Overseer," said the other soldier. "Overseer Osric. Now, back inside with you."

Ethan backed into the house. This could not be happening! How had Osric's part in all of this been covered up so quickly? Unless...yes, Osric must have had the aid of his supporters, whoever *they* were. Perhaps two of them stood outside the door. What could he do now? He could only wait. Ethan strode back up the stairs in a daze.

Jukes was really dead. It was hard to believe. Before his death he had approved of Ethan and Delia's friendship for the very first time. How ironic the whole thing was. Jukes having been directed by Osric somehow. How tragic that the man had just begun to consider the Creator. Tears formed in Ethan's eyes. He couldn't think about it any longer. Delia needed his help and there was still the mystery of the voice in his head. The voice that had been helping him, pushing him toward the answer found in the Brother Moons. But how was it possible that the old voice was inside his head. Wait...the *old* voice...no, the *ancient* voice. It was speaking to him! The Ancient that Maridia sat on top of must have been trying to help him. He wasn't crazy after all. But how did the Ancient know the exact date of the conjunction? How could Ethan find out?

Maridian's hadn't studied the stars like the Celestions of Glæm. It had been too close to Gloam and too the clouds for such research. There was no way for him to know the date. Unless...

"Er...when is the conjunction of the Brother Moons?" asked Ethan. He felt foolish like he was talking to a wall.

"This very day," rose a deep voice in his mind.

"Are you an Ancient?" Ethan had to be sure.

"I am."

"But...then why didn't you make yourself clear?"

"I did."

"You didn't tell me when the conjunction was before," said Ethan frustrated now.

"You did not ask."

Ethan smiled despite himself. It appeared that this Ancient had a sense of humor; or, at the very least, the old creature's mind did not work like his.

"Thank you," said Ethan.

"You are welcome, Child of the foretold."

"Child of the foretold? Does this have something to do with the Seer?" said Ethan, remembering the words of the last Ancient that had spoken to him.

"In time, all we be known."

A sense of humor and mysterious...

Now Ethan knew that the conjunction was upon him. But what good would this do if he couldn't get to Osric in time? Frustrated, Ethan plopped down on his bed and began to consider his options. After a good hour he'd come up with...nothing.

Later there was a knock at the door. Curious, Ethan was off to answer it. Before he'd made it down the stairs, the Healer came barging in.

"I know, I know," said the man. "I won't be but a few minutes. Someone, qualified, needs to check on Deerborn's wife."

The old man eyed Ethan and went straight to work in the kitchen mixing up some sort of concoction.

"What are you making there?" asked one of the soldiers.

"Well, only the best soup money can buy," said the Healer. "It's for Abril. I make it every day for her. Nothing more healthy or more tasty, I might add."

The Healer didn't make soup for Abril. She couldn't even take soup. What was going on?

"How 'bout a taste," said the other guard, reaching out for the spoon.

"Now, hold on just a sec," said the Healer slapping away the man's hand.

The guard looked taken aback.

"*I know* it's chilly out there. Once the soup is done I'll give you fellas a taste."

The soldiers eyed one another and went back to their post, leaving the door standing wide open, the brisk air filling up the room.

The Healer winked at Ethan.

From time to time, the guards would peek in to make sure nothing out of the ordinary was happening. But what they didn't realize was that the whole thing was out of the ordinary. Finally, the Healer declared the soup to be finished, which brought the guards in from their post.

"Here you go, men," said the Healer. "Two cups, just for you."

The men took the cups and buried their faces in them.

"Enjoy," said the Healer, smiling mischievously. "You're going to want move, Ethan."

"What? Why?"

But the answer landed on him. One of the soldiers fell straight towards Ethan, pinning him to the ground. The other was caught by the Healer and dragged to the kitchen table. Ethan pulled himself out from under the man.

"Did you just...poison them?" asked Ethan.

"Poison is too strong a word," said the Healer. "But, perhaps, I did poison them a little. I put them to sleep."

"For how long?"

"A few hours at the most."

"Osric will lock you up for sure."

"I'll deal with that. You've got to get out of town."

"I can't."

"You can't? Now listen: Jury and I didn't come up with this plan just to see it go to waste."

"Professor Jury helped you with this?" asked Ethan excitedly.

"Helped me? It was her idea!"

"Then I'll go to *her*."

"You can't. The town is teeming with folks preparing for Jukes' funeral. Most of them know you're under house arrest," said the Healer.

"The funeral is today?"

"It is," said the Healer. "This evening, in fact."

"Can you help me undress this man?" asked Ethan.

"Can I help you what? Oh, I see. You want his armor."

Ethan nodded. He was already bent over the guard that had fallen on him.

"A smart young man, you are."

"Thanks, uh...what's your name, anyway?" asked Ethan.

"Vanklavarhoefen," said the Healer.

"Van...what?"

"Don't bother...that's why I'm just referred to as the Healer."

Ethan found reason to smile as the Healer helped him suit up in the garb of a Maridian Guard. Minutes later, Ethan was out the door, a plan forming in his mind.

Chapter Twenty Six
For the Sake of the Many

Maridia was just as the Healer had said it would be. People were hustling and bustling all around town. Ethan saw that the Maridian Guard was everywhere. He hadn't known Maridia had so many soldiers. Maybe all of the guards had been placed on duty for the funeral. Maybe the new Overseer had promoted his supporters into the ranks of the guard. Maybe both were true. Ethan pulled his helmet down closer to his eyes to better hide his face. He knew where he was going; he just had to get there. As he was reaching the fountain, he spotted Osric at the entrance to Mikael's shop. He was yelling at the blacksmith. Something about a new order of weapons. Ethan realized something that he should have already considered. There were no guards in front of Deerborn's home now. Looking back, Ethan smiled proudly to see that the Healer had donned the other suit of armor and was pretending to be a guard at the front door. While he was looking back, he continued to move forward causing him to run into something. Startled, he turned to find his face buried in black robes. Ethan knew immediately who he'd run into. A forceful grip took hold of his shoulders.

"Watch where you're going soldier," growled Osric.

"Sorry, sir," replied Ethan in as deep a voice as he could muster. Ethan kept his head down.

"No harm done," said the Overseer. "Carry on. We have a busy evening ahead of us."

"Yes, sir," said Ethan. He'd almost ruined everything in a moment of carelessness.

Slipping through the congested street filled with carpenters, florists, painters, and the like, Ethan discovered just how big a production Osric was going to make out of Jukes' funeral. How ironic, that he had been the very person to end the rightful Overseer's life-- even though no one knew it. Ethan was determined to change that, though. Even if he couldn't prove that Osric had killed Jukes, he'd do everything in his power to show the town what their new leader was really like. He knew that revealing the Light of Glæm, in the presence of every living Maridian would send Osric into a maddened frenzy; or, at least he hoped it would.

Finally, Ethan made it to the other side of the town and safely slipped beneath the sign that read THE WAY TO KNOWLEDGE. He'd gone directly into the hornet's nest. Traveling quickly down the lamp-lit corridor, he passed the marble reliefs for what would probably be one of the last times. He climbed the stairs, two at a time, and sprinted towards the very last classroom down the left hall.

"Professor Jury!" shouted Ethan, flinging the door open, wide.

The room was deserted. As he was turning to leave, Ethan heard a muffled cry from the back of the room. It was coming from the open door that led down the stairs to J. Jury's office. Ethan took off towards the door. Entering her study he found yet another empty room; but he could still hear the cries. They were coming from behind the wall. Ethan found the professor bound and gagged in the secret library behind her desk.

"What happened?" asked Ethan as he untied the woman's fetters.

Breathing deeply, Professor Jury said, "When news spread that Jukes' had been killed and that you were being detained, I went to the Healer with a plan to help you."

"It worked," smiled Ethan.

"I see that," returned J. Jury.

"How did you know you could trust the Healer?" asked Ethan, still curious about who was actually on Osric's side.

"It is no secret that that man despises Osric. Let's just say I took a chance on him."

"Then what happened?"

"Then I came back to my study to begin packing up all of these books."

Ethan looked perplexed.

"I knew that if Osric became the Overseer he'd search every corner of every building in the citadel to find and destroy these works," explained J. Jury. "Then...then he found me here. I didn't think he was capable of such hatred."

She began to cry.

Ethan placed a hand on her back. "It's okay. We'll get the books out of here but first we have to make sure the rest of the town knows what Osric is really like. I have a plan to do just that."

Ethan explained about the coming alignment of the moons and of the momentary darkness that would accompany the phenomena. To ready the professor for what the town would witness, he closed the door to the hidden room enveloping them in darkness, but only for a moment. Ethan removed the helmet, pulled up his sleeves, and the little room was showered in a radiant glow. J. Jury gasped and a look akin to fear briefly past over her face. Ethan opened the door up again and shared the rest of his plan. He would need her help in getting Deerborn and Blaise out of their cells. He didn't think that any of the guards could be trusted at this point, so he suggested that she acquire the help of Mikael Temujin. Ethan explained that most of the guards seemed to be at work in the streets. This might make it easier to get to Deerborn, especially if she and Mikael could find Blaise first. He knew exactly where The Captain of the Maridian Guard was being held. The plan seemed as solid as anything the professor might have come up with and so she agreed to it. Ethan gave the woman his armor to pose as a guard, making it easier for her to get to Mikael; then, she gave Ethan one of her black professor's robes that looked exactly like Osric's. She was shorter than Ethan, making the robes too small, but this would matter little. Soon Ethan would be shedding the robes for the sake of Deerborn and Abril, for the sake of Delia and the memory of her father, for the sake of J. Jury, Mikael, the Healer, and all the Maridians that would fall prey to the whims of so evil an Overseer as Osric. Mostly Ethan would shed the robes for the sake of his faith and his Creator.

Professor Jury finished dressing in the armor, but before she left she said, "Ethan, there's one more thing I have to tell you. Before I confronted Osric, I overheard him talking with someone in his study."

"I thought he was talking to himself," said Ethan.

"Jukes told you that?" asked the Professor.

"Yes...just before he was murdered," said Ethan.

"Well, unfortunately I didn't tell Jukes everything I heard. I was afraid to say it at the time."

"Who was Osric talking to?"

"I'm not sure, but there was an un-human sounding voice in the room with him."

"But didn't you tell Jukes that Osric was alone?"

"He was! When he opened the door there was no one else in the room with him."

"I don't understand," said Ethan.

"Neither do I," replied J. Jury.

"What did the voice say?" asked Ethan.

"It said it was finished dealing with him. I suppose it meant Osric. It said that he had lost his hold on the situation. It sounded angry! I was afraid, Ethan. But, if I had told Jukes everything, he might not have...died."

"I don't think it would have mattered, Professor. Jukes would have still confronted the Rector."

"I know, but he might have been more prepared. Hopefully, you might be more prepared, now."

"Thanks, Professor."

"Be safe, Ethan."

"You, too."

Professor Jury ran out, leaving Ethan to his thoughts. He wasn't sure what this news meant, but he had his suspicions and he didn't like them. No matter...the plan was in action now.

Where have you been, friend?

Chapter Twenty Seven
The Conjunction

Ethan went back upstairs, to the opposite side of the university, and found a place to wait. He needed to watch for the lunar alignment and Snow Beast's classroom had several windows that overlooked the center of town. It would work perfectly from there. Rows of strung lantern's flickered high above the ground, making the town-center look more like the spot of a coming celebration rather than a funeral. Perhaps that was the way of the Maridians: to celebrate a life rather than a death. Either way, the few prep teams that remained outside hadn't yet noticed the Brother Moons slowly converging above. This was to be expected. To the Maridians, just being able to see the moons at all was a spectacle in and of itself. On his right, Ethan could see a stage set up in front of the Overseer's home. He squinted hard at Jukes' windows in hopes of spotting any sign of Delia. There was nothing.

After a short time the crowds began to form again, though much more orderly than before. The funeral would begin soon. There was still a little time before the conjunction, though. The long wait gave Ethan time to ponder thoughts that he'd not yet had time to consider. He'd been so busy. What if his plan went horribly wrong? How many people would suffer for his oversights, his carelessness? He had to time everything just right. Any of his accomplices would surely be put to death otherwise. *He* might be caught and put to death. The thought of never seeing his family again hadn't really occurred to him until this moment but it was a real possibility. No...he didn't have time to consider these thoughts any longer. He must be brave. Ethan prayed that his plan would work. The time finally came for him to make his move. The conjunction was at hand.

He ran to the classroom door and directly into Professor Fleming. The plumpish man adjusted his spectacles to see with whom he'd collided. His comical appearance truly defied the genius of his mind.

"Oh...hello, Mr. Lambent," said Snow Beast, rubbing a hand through his fuzzy white hair. "What are you doing in my classroom at this hour? Don't you know the funeral is beginning?"

"Yes, sir," replied Ethan. "I was just..."

"And what are you doing in those robes?" interrupted the man.

"I am supposed to say something at the funeral and I didn't have the appropriate clothing for the occasion," said Ethan, uncomfortable at the lie but he didn't know what else to say. He wasn't sure whether or not this man was friend or foe.

"Speaking at the funeral, huh?"

"Um...yes, sir." Ethan felt awful about deceiving the man.

"Well then, you'd better run along or you'll miss your chance."

"Thank you, sir, I'll see you down there."

"Yes, yes...see you there."

The professor's thoughts seemed to be elsewhere.

Heart racing, Ethan took off down the hallway. Soon he was in the street among the spectators. There were so many people. He looked up and saw that two of the moons were already becoming crescents that slowly began to block out the sun. He'd been detained by Professor Fleming for too long. Ethan looked towards the guard house in hopes of seeing any sign of friends. They hadn't yet emerged, if they were to at all. Ethan couldn't think about that right now. He was determined to do this with or without anyone's help. Deerborn's front door was now blocked by the crowd, which made it impossible to know if the Healer still stood guard there. From somewhere a song began to ring out and the crowd joined in. He'd need to get to the stage so that everyone, Osric most of all, would have a clear view of him. The song that the crowd sang sounded similar to the tunes that Watts had hummed in the past. He was sure Watts was still posted at the Eastern Lookout and wouldn't be attending the ceremony. He would have made a great ally; but, no time to lament about that now. The crowd got thicker as Ethan drew closer to the front. With a fleeting thought, Ethan wondered if the dangling lanterns would be bright enough to weaken the coming effect. Finally, he could see the stage in its entirety. First he saw the coffin of Alaric Jukes and then, to his utter shock, he saw Delia sitting slumped on the stage right next to Osric. He couldn't understand why she wasn't trying to attack her father's killer like she had earlier. The closer Ethan pressed, the better he could see Delia. Her eyes bore the same type of dark circles around them as Osric's. Had he gotten into her mind like he had Jukes? The thought infuriated Ethan and he pushed forward with more force. People began peering back for the source of the commotion and a few of them gasped when they saw Ethan. He found Jocelyn near the stage and went towards her. Her wide-eyes met his and he held his finger to his mouth in hopes of keeping her quiet. It worked; she didn't betray him. He edged in close to her to better hide himself.

"What are you doing here?" whispered the young woman. "I thought you were under house arrest."

"I am," answered Ethan, but that was all he had time to say. The song ended and Osric rose from his seat.

The new Overseer raised his hands to silence the crowd and this time it worked immediately.

"We are here to remember the life of one who served this city with greatness. Not only he but his fore-fathers before him. We also gather today to look, hopefully, toward a new era and a new lineage of Overseers. Such has not happened in centuries, but let us not forget that it was the man who we lay low today that bestowed upon me the honor of Regent. Therefore, it is only fitting that we respect our dearly departed's choice, nay even his vision for the future."

Some cheered, but it could have very well been out of fear. Ethan could not tell.

His thoughts were in two places at once-- on his plan and on his friend sitting on the stage. He looked towards the Brothers, seeing the event would happen soon, then he looked at Delia. What had happened to her? The Rector stopped in mid-sentence. He was in huddled conversation with another man. Another man wearing the same black robes...

Osric straightened and looked directly at Ethan. Professor Fleming was standing beside Osric pointing at the Glæmian. Snow Beast's comical appearance had been more deceiving than Ethan had known. The teacher was one of Osric's supporters!

"Bring the boy up here!" shouted Osric.

The crowd pushed Ethan towards the front. Two soldiers on the stage yanked him on to the platform. Delia looked up, unconcerned. He'd made it to the stage but not in the way he wanted to.

"People of Maridia," began Osric. "Before you stands an outsider."

Osric moved smoothly toward Ethan. The man's eyes had gone completely white but for his deep-black pupils. They bore a familiar darkness. His face was now skin on bone, nothing more.

A few in the crowd taunted and jeered at Ethan. Miss Naava brought a book down on one of their heads, silencing them instantly.

"Not only is he an outsider but it is believed that he is a conspirator in the murder of Alaric Jukes!" shouted Osric, now so close to the Glæmian's face that Ethan could see his rotting teeth and smell his rancid breath. Osric had brought death and he reeked of it, as well.

Somewhere in the crowd a Maridian shouted curses at Ethan. His words sounded much like those of the Luminae folk who hated Canis so.

"So, now I ask you good people of Maridia, what should we do with this conspirator?"

"Kick him out!" said one.

"Lock him away!" said another.

"Now, now," replied Osric. "Let us be civil about this."

The Overseer grabbed Ethan by the collar.

"As a show of good faith, we shall allow the accused to defend himself. So what say you Ethan Lambent of Glæm?"

Osric raised his hand and again the crowd fell silent.

Ethan peered skyward one last time and smiled.

"Blaise did not kill Jukes, Osr..."

Osric's large, damp hand clasped Ethan's mouth shut.

Somewhere in the crowd a solitary scream rent the air as the mountain-top city began to grow dark. Other cries joined, as people pointed towards the moons.

Vergance, Miland, and Ancelin appeared to collide with each other in the sky above. A strong gust of wind blew through the city, extinguishing the flickering lanterns. A darkness like that of Gloam fell over the land.

Disoriented by the sudden chaos, Osric lost his grip on Ethan. The Glæmian tore loose the robe from his shoulders revealing his glowing torso.

Now some were screaming and pointing at him, but there was another scream that overpowered all the rest. It was coming from Osric. A chill ran through Ethan as he realized that he'd heard this scream before, just as he'd seen those black eyes. He knew it now. Both were present on the night he'd Awakened.

Ethan's light was shining directly on Osric but the Overseer didn't look the same anymore. His body had contorted towards the ground and like a wild beast rearing up on his haunches, the thing lunged.

Leaping into the crowd, Ethan tried, frantically, to get away from the demon that had once been Osric. The throng of people below him moved aside as he leapt, none wanting to expose themselves to his illuminated body. He slammed hard into the ground and the people between him and the stage began to scatter as the nightmarish creature charged towards Ethan. Now, there was nothing between him and it. Osric was running on all fours, much like the Watchers had and much like the Watchers, it began to speak to Ethan.

"Did you think you could escape me, boy!" growled the abomination, slowing down to walk like man again. Its joints were bending in abnormal places, not where Osric's joints had been. If the Rector was still in there, he was in unbearable pain.

The head that had once belonged to the man was now bobbing loosely on the spine. His head was almost lifeless but for the disturbing way in which the lips moved, like they were guided by an outside force, like in Ethan's dream. His nightmare had come to life.

The thing pounced on Ethan and, with its broken and brittle fingers, it began to choke the life out of him.

From somewhere in the chaotic congestion that was the people of Maridia, a war cry went up and suddenly the creature was no longer on Ethan. A flash of light had passed quickly over him, relieving him of his assailant. It was another Glæmian. Whoever the glowing person was, he had locked himself around the beast that scraped and clawed the ground, trying desperately to crawl back towards Ethan.

The only discernible feature on the glowing figure was a beard.

"Father?" called Ethan as he inched closer to the stand off.

But it wasn't Amory. It was The Captain of The Maridian Guard.

Deerborn had Awakened! But when? Over a fortnight ago, of course. That explained why no one was able to see the man. Osric hadn't wanted anyone to know what had happened to him.

In the crowd, soldier stood off against soldier. Some had come to aid Deerborn, Blaise leading them on. Some were still loyal to Osric.

"Give up! Child-of-the-mountains!" mocked the creature, squeezing ever tighter at Deerborn's torso. Its piercing eyes were still locked on Ethan.

"I no longer belong to these hills," said Deerborn, applying equal pressure. "I am child of Glæm now!"

Deerborn screamed with rage and bones cracked within the creature. What had been Osric suddenly seized up like a dead spider and moved no more.

Deerborn released his bear-like grip on the beast. As he did the thing began to laugh. It was Smarr's laugh; there was no doubt.

"You can destroy this body. It is nothing more than an instrument," wheezed the wicked one with eyes only for Ethan. "There are many other instruments at my disposal. But soon, I will come for you, Lambent boy, and it will not be in the constraints of a human body that I seek you out!"

Gurgling overcame the monster and Smarr's words faded as the last drops of life were squeezed from his puppet--Rector Osric.

The conjunction was coming to an end and the sky was brightening again.

Deerborn and Ethan embraced.

"You're...you're..." began Ethan.

"Like you," finished Deerborn. "It was only a matter of time."

"But Abril, she's still in a coma," said Ethan.

"It will soon pass...I know it," said Deerborn confidently.

"Ethan! Deerborn!"

Delia was running straight for them and she looked every bit herself again. She joined in their embrace and soon others came. First, Mikael, then, J. Jury, and finally even the Healer. He had a severe gash across his face and needed a physician himself now.

"What happened to you, Healer?" asked Ethan.

"He saved my life," said Blaise, joining the group. "Took a sword to the face for me, that one did. The uprising has been put down, sir."

"Very good, soldier. Thank you for your help."

Blaise nodded, eyes glistening.

"Make way, make way for an old woman!" said another familiar voice pushing through the stunned crowd. It was Miss Naava. "Well, can't say I've ever seen anything quite like that b'fore!"

Some laughed, others, like Ethan and Delia, just stood and held on to one another.

Delia had a far off look about her. She was staring glassy-eyed at the stage where the body of her father lay, unsuspecting of anything that had just occurred in the city he once ruled over.

"We were in the middle of a funeral, weren't we?" said Ethan, speaking up so that all could hear. "I believe it is time to finish paying our respects."

Those who were left in the streets nodded their consent. No one seemed ready to accuse Ethan any longer.

"Aye, young man," said Deerborn. "Let's do just that."

A sadness rested in Deerborn's countenance. He'd not known until his release that his Overseer had been slain. His pain was fresh.

Soon, the funeral had begun again and a reverent hush fell over the proceedings.

Ethan had returned to the stage with Delia and Deerborn , who stood to say a few words.

But, those words never came. The voice of Blaise rose up near the guard house at the city gates.

"Watts? Are you okay?"

Everyone turned to see Watts stumble through the gate.

Watts looked sadly towards Blaise with some sort of horrible pain in his eyes.

"Where have you been, friend?" asked Blaise.

"The...the Eastern Lookout. They are coming..." were his lasts words. Abruptly, Watts fell to the ground never to rise again.

THE END

OF

STIRRING

BOOK TWO OF

THE EMBLEM AND THE LANTERN

TO BE CONTINUED

IN

GLOAMING

BOOK THREE OF

THE EMBLEM AND THE LANTERN

End Notes:

1. Most of the Gloamers' society revolves around song. For instance, their governments are a rudimentary aristocracy linked to singing ability-- the better one sings, the higher one's place in society. Families of the best singers remain in power, provided that their abilities are passed on to younger generations. In the event that they are not, the family's place in society is stripped from them. Gloamers also have songs to represent each family, much like a family crest. These songs serve as a surname as well. When the dark-dwellers encounter one another in the darkness, they often sing their family song to identify themselves. The sense of touch is prominent, as well. Ethan experienced this firsthand when the Restorer of By Down treated his injured leg. The pale man gave a diagnosis of the injury without looking upon Ethan's leg even once. Textures also played a major part in daily life. Historically, Gloamers have spent a considerable amount of time developing clothing that is interesting to the touch. Color and shape are of little importance, but texture is everything.

2. In Ethan's lifetime, theories about the heavens began to change. At one time, all Glæmians believed the blue sky was the ceiling of Glæm and the floor of the Creator's realm. This made sense; the heavenly lights that lit the world were steered across the sky by day and by night. It was as if the Creator, Himself, was in control of these bodies

from his realm above. Another widely held belief was that the stars were simply pinpricks in the ceiling of the world, showing tiny glimpses into the heavenly country on the other side. It was once believed that the moons possessed a light of their own. But with the study of the lunar eclipse, Celestions (or experts of the skies) deduced that because the moons grew darker during these events they must reflect the light of the sun rather than bearing lights of their own. New ideas about the stars formed from these theories, as well, such as the possibility of the heavenly bodies being like Glæm's sun, only much further away.

3. Ethan's map of Gloam:

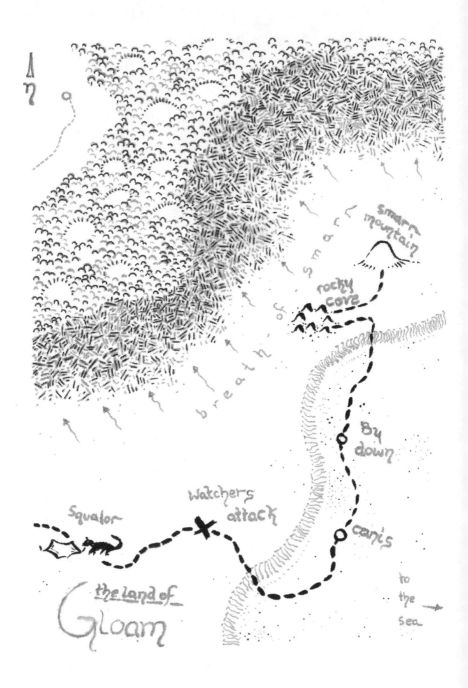

ABOUT THE AUTHOR

Dylan Higgins is a husband, father, son, brother, friend, pastor, teacher, student, storyteller, singer / songwriter and graphic designer, among other things.

Dylan and his family dwell in Brooks, Georgia in a house called *Spalding's End*, having been built many decades ago on the edge of the county bearing the same name. As it happens, Dylan's wife grew up in this very home just as their children are currently doing.

Dylan is a member of the indie folk band *Sleepy Turtles* on Autumn + Colour Records™. The songs in this book are on their recent release called *Summer, Hither*.

www.sleepyturtlesmusic.com

ABOUT THE ILLUSTRATOR

Mikael Jury is a student at Belhaven University in Mississippi. In addition to being an illustrator, Mikael is a fine blacksmith, who has actually forged the Magic Lantern in his smithy. Mikael and Dylan are a part of the same church community, where their legendary partnership, in this series, first began!

ACKNOWLEDGEMENTS

Thank you to the following. I am continually amazed by the adventure we are on together! First, to my beautiful wife who, being pregnant with our third child, has put up with an unfair share of days apart from me so that I could complete this book! Thank you for your sacrifice my love; to Ethan and Eisley who continue to be the inspiration for *The Emblem and The Lantern*! God has made you both far more amazing in reality than I could ever make you in a fiction; to Mikael Jury: your illustrations have the ability to bring me to tears. I will never understand how you can pull what I'm imagining right out of my head! Further up and further in my friend. (I hope you like your character!); to Joanna Jury, for your editing and for continuing in this journey with me! (I hope you liked your character, too, professor!); to Barbara Toth, for making yourself available to aid in the editing process; to the Ink Slingers: Josh Campbell, Jon Cooper, Mikael Jury, and Mike Sherrard. Together we hone the craft; to Clay Parker for your film work yet again! Still waiting on that movie; to the Sleepy Turtles who brought the songs in the book to life again; to Autumn + Colour Records™ for all the promotion; to all the parents, schools, and churches that have allowed me to share my stories and music with your students: The Campus, Rising Starr Middle, Peeples Elementary, Skipstone Academy, and Crosspoint Church, to name a few; to Omega Books for being the first book store to sell my novels; to Forrest Shultz for reviewing *Stirring* in manuscript form; to the Lost Genre Guild for welcoming me into your community like you have; to George MacDonald (Dòmhnall) for paving the way; to all those who have read or will read this series: I hope it continues to inspire you and cause you to ask question that matter; to my Savior, Jesus Christ, whose unrelenting love for me renders me speechless!

AN EXCERPT FROM

GLOAMING

BOOK THREE OF

THE EMBLEM AND THE LANTERN

* * *

Eisley awoke, rolled out of bed, and dressed for her run. She started for her brother's room, like so many mornings before but turned in mid-stride, shaking her head at herself. Old habits were hard to break. Ethan was gone. He had been gone for weeks and still she rose each day expecting her brother to be there, to run with her. She walked to the sink and poured herself a small glass of water, quickly turning it up and downing it. Marching out onto the front porch and down to the lawn, Eisley stopped and stretched toward the deep blue morning sky.

As Eisley began to run, the autumn air swept across her face; a pleasant welcome to a new day. Cold tears streamed back towards her hairline. Was she crying; or, was it the chilly air that made her eyes water so? If her thoughts were any indication, it was tears. Eisley looked to were Ethan normally ran beside her and felt a deep longing for him. She missed their runs, she missed his laugh, but most of all she just missed his company. They'd been together since birth, but no longer. How was he? Had they arrived in Maridia safely? Had he seen Jukes and Delia? Had he started classes yet? What classes was he taking? So many questions that could not be answered. Mail did not run from Luminae to Maridia and so she didn't know what was happening in her brother's life. This upset her. She was sure that he must feel the same way, not knowing what was happening at home. At least he was in good company. For that Eisley was thankful. She was also grateful that she had Canis to talk to, though his words were few.

Canis was good company, but of a different kind than her brother. She could always tell what Ethan was thinking because he constantly showed it in his expressions. Canis, on the other hand, remained, for the most part, expressionless. Eisley could never get a handle on his thoughts. This bothered her, because her family was so animated, especially Grandpa Emmett! Likewise, Ethan always talked about what was on his mind and there was *always* something on his mind. Canis, though, only spoke when he really had something to say. Eisley appreciated this because she knew that if Canis did speak it was worth hearing.

Running into town, she noticed more activity than normal on the square. The stages were being repainted by a team of men whose trousers were covered in old hardened paint. Eisley thought it would make their uniforms very uncomfortable to wear day in and day out. The shops were much busier, as well. She ran around a long line formed outside Bon's Bakery. Waving at the stream of new faces Eisley said, "Good morning," in a breathless voice as she passed. The bakery smelled of chocolate covered goodness and she wished that she'd brought her change purse along. It wasn't often that the bakery's door stood wide open to taunt her with its pleasant smells from within. But when the Awakening crowd came to town, Bon's was always a favorite morning destination. Mrs. Bon kept the doors opened to draw the helpless visitors in. Eisley knew that behind her and down the hill a ways, South Main Street was a bustle of activity. Families were buying their beloved memorabilia for the coming celebration, only a few days away.

Since Ethan's departure, the Lambents had laid low, not going into town very often in order to refrain from unnecessary confrontation. Eisley was glad of this because she didn't want a repeat of that dreadful morning when Ethan had lost it in front the township. Luckily, no one seemed to pay her any mind. Perhaps she ran by too quickly for anyone to say anything. If she'd taken the time to stop and listen, she would have heard people muttering in hushed voices with one another about those, "mischievous Lambents who invite whomever they please into town from strange lands beyond." But Eisley would have shown little concern. She ran on in what would have been complete jubilation if not for the absence of her brother. She passed the town stables where she decided to stop and pet all the horses belonging to those who'd made long journeys to Luminae. After a few minutes of speaking with the animals she fell back into a comfortable jog, headed for home.

***

"Let'em try something, I'll..." yelled Grandpa Emmett who was apparently in quite a tizzy over something that Eisley suspected to be related to Canis.

"What's the matter Grandpa?"

"Your mother can explain it!" said Emmett as he passed Eisley, tromping off into the front yard and down the way. Eisley heard him mumbling to himself as he went.

"Uh-oh," said Eisley opening the screen door. "What now?"

Evangeline sighed and plopped down in a chair in the sitting room. "Grandpa's just getting worked up over nothing. That's all."

Eisley came and rested on the arm of the chair where her mother sat. She thought that her mother looked a bit too tired for so early in the morning. "Does it have to do with Canis then?"

"Of course," Evangeline said looking up at Eisley and kissing her on the arm. "I say your grandpa's getting worked up over nothing, but that might just be wishful thinking."

Evangeline wiped sweat from her brow and breathed a little deeper than normal.

"Are you alright, mother?"

"Yes, child, a little under the weather today is all. Anyways," said Evangeline changing the subject, "Canis wants to participate in the Awakening."

Eisley didn't say anything and immediately she knew that her mother *was* only wishful thinking. If Canis was a participant in the ceremonies there would most definitely be trouble. Eisley was sure her mother knew this as well. Evangeline had simply grown tired of all the confrontation and hoped for better days in the town she loved so much. Thus far, her mother had taken everything with an air of grace. This was the first time Eisley had noticed it wearing on her. Or was it even the news that had her mother looking so worn?

"Are you sure you're okay?" asked Eisley again, when her mother's brow furrowed in pain.

"I'm fine, Eisley girl," said Evangeline, standing to kiss Eisley on the forehead. "Just feeling a little queazy this morning." Then she sauntered off toward the kitchen.

Soon Eisley knew she'd be adding to her mother's frustration, when she mustered the courage to tell Evangeline that she was going back to Gloam. She hoped that her mother was in better spirits on that day because she would need the reserve. Turning her thoughts to Canis, she got up and went to Ethan's room where Canis was now staying. Eisley knocked on the door and waited. No one answered. She cracked the door open and called his name. Again, there was no answer so she opened the door to find the room empty, the bed neatly made. Ethan's room seemed desolate because he had taken most of his things with him. The walls were bare, the desktop was empty and the wardrobe hung open slightly, revealing a dark vacantness that had once been filled by Ethan's clothes.

Only a solitary brown, tunic hung where there had once been many. Eisley sighed at the sad sight, walked over to the window above Ethan's desk, and peered out into the bright morning. Her father was saddling Lewis. Canis was helping him. They seemed to be deep in conversation.

Eisley went to meet them, interrupting their talk. Canis noticed her first and stopped in mid-sentence to bid Eisley good morning. She returned the greeting and neared her father, kissing his bewhiskered cheek.

"Good Morning, Daddy," she said.

"Morning, Love," said Amory.

"Where are you going?" asked Eisley, as Amory mounted the farm horse.

"To try and calm your grandpa down."

"Good luck," she said in earnest.

Amory ran his fingers across Eisley's cheek and smiled down at her. Without another word he trotted off to find his father.

"The Awakening ceremony, huh?" said Eisley, still watching Lewis carry her father down the road.

"Yes," said Canis.

"But, why?" said Eisley, turning to look at the young man. "The ceremony isn't even all that important. It's the decision you've already made that really matters."

"I feel differently about the matter," said Canis. "Where I come from the ceremony is as much a part of the decision as the decision itself. It is a public showing of one's choice...of one's commitment."

"I've never thought of it like that before," said Eisley, pondering the idea. It brought thoughts of her own Awakening ceremony to mind. "We...Ethan and I, I mean, we had our ceremony in the wood just behind our home. I don't suppose you'd consider doing that would you?"

"A decent notion, but I'm afraid not," he began. "I've been thinking about this for quite some time. Even though I've passed the appropriate age, I believe it is my duty to the Creator, even my privilege, to participate in the Awakening." Canis glanced skyward. "I have even wondered if this would not help my standing in Glæm. To make public, once and for all, what I stand for and Whom I stand for."

Eisley considered the idea. She wasn't sure whether or not it would work. She could only hope it would, because she was unsure of how much more of this conflict she could take.

HILL HAROW BOOKS™

Made in the USA
Charleston, SC
17 May 2013